VEIL, VOWS and VENGEANCE

EMERALD FINN

FINESSE SOLUTIONS

Cover design by Wicked Good Book Designs
Published by Finesse Solutions Pty Ltd
2022/04/30
ISBN: 9781925607093

Author's note: This book was written and produced in Australia and uses British/Australian spelling conventions, such as "colour" instead of "color", and "-ise" endings instead of "-ize" on words like "realise".

A catalogue record for this book is available from the National Library of Australia

For Jen, my criminally minded daughter

CHAPTER 1

I ALWAYS CRIED AT WEDDINGS. EVEN IF I BARELY KNEW THE HAPPY couple—and, apparently, even if I was supposed to be working. Weddings were such emotional occasions—all that joy and love was too much for me at the best of times. And these were definitely not the best of times. With the date of my own cancelled wedding barely two months away, and my cheating ex-fiancé deluging me with unwelcome flowers, my emotions were all over the joint.

Hastily wiping away tears, I peered through my lens and zoomed in on the bride's face as she said her *I do's* on the sand. This was my first big job as a brand-new professional photographer, and I would *not* screw this up. I had big plans for Charlie Carter Photography. With the beautiful blue sea bringing out the blue of the bride's eyes, and the sun warm on the golden sand of Sunrise Bay, this beach wedding was going to look amazing on my shiny new website.

Molly was wearing a simple style that could have been

1

a sundress if it hadn't been made of white lace, and her blond hair was up in a loose bun with a few curls hanging down by her ears. A crown of pale pink flowers sat atop a short veil. She looked fresh and pretty and absolutely perfect for a beach wedding.

You'd never guess from her current sweet appearance how badly she'd been behaving all afternoon, ordering her bridesmaids around as if they were sixteenth-century serfs and complaining about everything from the smell of the flowers—overpowering, apparently—to the brand of champagne—too cheap. By the time I'd finished taking photos of the bride and her attendants getting ready, each of the bridesmaids had been in tears at least once.

There'd been a distinct possibility that Molly wouldn't make it to the altar, because if she'd kept it up much longer, I would have killed her myself. My book club friend Sarah, who was Molly's sister and matron of honour, had whispered an apology to me for her sister's behaviour as we were leaving the house for the ceremony.

"Sorry Molly's being a bit of a harpy. It's the nerves. She can't help it."

Privately, I thought that she could have helped it if she wanted to, and "harpy" was probably Molly's default setting. My Aunt Evie would have had a few choice words to say to her on the matter if she'd been here—so it was just as well for the sake of my fledgling business that she wasn't. I could put up with a few tantrums.

Her bridesmaids wore strapless dresses that fell just below their knees, in the same blue as the perfect cloudless sky, and the two cute flower girls were in organza dresses in a lighter blue that made them look like little fairies. The men wore white shirts and trousers rolled up at the ankle, with tan jackets over the top. Everyone's feet were bare. It all looked casual and beach-chic.

Molly and her new husband Marco exchanged rings, and I made sure to get close-ups of them sliding the golden bands onto each other's fingers. Each band was made of entwined strands of white, rose, and yellow gold, matching the beautiful filigree and diamond engagement ring Molly wore. I'd exclaimed over how unusual it was when I'd arrived at her house this afternoon, and she'd told me she had designed it herself.

I had a list of must-have shots for the day, and the exchange of rings was one of them. Another was their first kiss as a married couple, and I teared up again as Marco's dark head bent towards Molly's blond, flower-crowned one. She might have been a harpy, but it was still a beautiful moment. I just hoped Marco knew what he was getting himself into.

At least I wasn't the only one crying. Sarah was wiping under her eyes, careful not to smudge her mascara, the tantrums of the afternoon forgiven—or at least forgotten for now. I didn't know Sarah very well, having only spoken to her at book club meetings before, so I couldn't be sure. There were quite a few damp eyes among the guests, too, including the bride's mother and father, though that might have been relief that they were getting rid of her. A lady in the third row in a pink straw hat wasn't just sniffing back the odd tear. She was full-on crying, with tears running down her cheeks, and clearly *her* mascara wasn't waterproof. They didn't look like happy tears, either, and I hoped she was okay.

Once the first kiss was done, the crying part was over, at least for me. Now I could really focus on my job. The celebrant gave her final blessings, the late afternoon sun sparkled on the blue, blue water, and the guests cheered as the new Mr and Mrs Lombardi proceeded down the sandy aisle, all smiles.

Next stop: the golden sandstone cliffs at the southern end of the beach. They would make the perfect backdrop for some truly spectacular wedding photos.

Getting the bridal party there was like herding cats. Everyone wanted to talk to the new couple and congratulate them, and I gritted my teeth as guests surrounded them.

My friend Priya stopped beside me. "Nice day for it. Molly looks like an angel."

I glanced at her. She was looking very pretty in a figure-hugging emerald dress, her thick, dark hair swept up into a messy bun. A chunky gold bracelet adorned each wrist.

"Looks can be deceiving."

She grinned. "Bit of a bridezilla, is she? That checks out. I never liked her much. Sarah's definitely the pick of the Simpson girls."

"What are you doing at her wedding, then?"

"I'm a friend of Marco's. Don't let Molly push you around. She'll expect perfect photos, so you'll need to be the boss."

I nodded. "Did you bring a date?"

"No. Flying solo. And speaking of flying ... check out the hat." She nodded at a couple who were pushing their way through the crowd around the bride and groom. The man was short and compact and wearing a grey jacket despite the warm November weather, while the woman dripped with diamonds and had some kind of feathered confection on her head. She looked like she should be at the races, not a casual beach wedding. "One more feather and she'd be airborne."

I snorted, then cleared my throat. "Ladies and gents, there are champagne and canapes waiting for you upstairs in the surf club." Some of these people would hang around forever if I didn't give them a little nudge. "I need to steal the bridal party away for photos before we lose the light."

There wasn't much chance of that. It was just after six, and the sun wouldn't disappear until well after seven at this time of year. Daylight saving had already started and summer was just around the corner. But we were still on a tight timetable to get the official wedding photos.

Most of the crowd dutifully turned away, but the man in the grey jacket shoved his way through to Marco and Molly, pushing Sarah's husband Troy out of the way as he did. Troy wasn't in the bridal party, but he was hanging around chatting to Sarah. He turned to the man with a startled look that became a snarl.

"Watch it, Cassar." The man ignored him, stretching out his hand to shake hands with Marco, and Troy grabbed him by the shoulder and spun him around. "I'm talking to you."

I wasn't sure what happened next. The woman in the

5

feathered hat shrieked, and Sarah said, "Troy!" in an urgent undertone, and suddenly Troy was staggering backwards on the sand.

An ugly look crossed his face, and he leapt forward, fist swinging. Marco caught at the back of his shirt, but it was too late—the man in the grey jacket was on the ground, spitting sand out of his face. He surged up and suddenly the whole bridal party was in motion, the women scattering like a flock of frightened seagulls, and the men rushing forward, some to grab the man and some to grab Troy.

"Looks like Troy might have already started on the champagne," Priya said, cool as a cucumber. "You going to get photos of this?"

I cast her a withering look. As if any couple wanted mementoes of a brawl at their wedding. But it was over in a flash. Two of the groomsmen escorted a struggling Troy in the direction of the surf club, one on each arm.

"I'll see you later," Priya said, starting after them. That was the journalist in her—she smelled a good story, and I was sure it wouldn't take her long to ferret it out.

Marco helped the other man to his feet. He was perhaps fifty, with the pugnacious look of a boxer. He'd clearly been handsome in his youth and still had plenty of dark brown hair, but his nose looked as though it had been broken at some stage and he had a smug look that I didn't like. He brushed sand off his jacket ostentatiously while Molly and Marco fussed over him. By the time he'd finished shaking Marco's hand and kissing Molly with rather more enthusiasm than seemed appropriate, the two groomsmen had returned.

"If we could move on to the photos?" I suggested, and finally the man and his feathered wife took the hint and headed towards the surf club, where the reception was being held.

"I *hate* him," Sarah said to his departing back, as I got the bridal party moving down the beach towards the cliffs. "Why did you have to invite him?"

"Because he's Marco's boss," Molly hissed at her.

"But after everything he's done? I'm your sister."

"And Marco's my *husband*," Molly said. "He needs the job—we couldn't snub his boss. Can't you keep *your* stupid husband under control?"

"How about some shots here?" I cut in, before the argument intensified. I was learning that it was the wedding photographer's job to keep everybody happy. You couldn't get good photos without smiling faces.

We had reached the tumbled rocks at the base of the cliff. Further on, they formed a rock shelf that jutted out into the deeper water. At high tide, waves broke against the shelf, which would have made a spectacular backdrop, but it was low tide at the moment. Which was probably a good thing. Breaking waves might look spectacular, but we also ran the risk of ending up with a drenched bride and groom, which wouldn't make anybody happy.

I had the groom and his attendants roll up their trousers to the knee, then Marco swept Molly into his arms and waded into the water. It was very still at this sheltered south end of the beach, protected by the headland. Sarah, her face like stone, gathered up her own skirts and waded in far enough to hold Molly's veil out so that the diamantes on it sparkled in the sun. I snapped away, capturing the delight on Molly's face and the pride in Marco's eyes as he gazed at the woman in his arms. Hopefully Sarah's mood would improve before I had to take the group shots.

We spent some time on the beach getting pictures against the blue backdrop of the ocean. The two flower girls quickly got bored and started picking up shells. They looked about three and five, and were probably sisters judging by how similar they looked, with their big blue eyes and blond ringlets, now festooned with flower crowns. I kept half an eye on them in case they got too close to the water, but they became engrossed in some game that left them very sandy. At least they weren't wet. After that we trooped up onto the rocks and got some gorgeous shots against the warm colours of the cliffs in the soft afternoon light.

I could have kept shooting for hours—or at least until the light failed—but I was conscious of the surf club's timetable. They wanted to start serving dinner at seven. They'd need the bridal party back for that, so I kept one eye on my watch as I ordered everyone around, making sure to get all the shots on the list of highlights that I'd prepared. Beach weddings were a lot of fun to shoot, as it turned out. The groomsmen clowned around, keeping the bridesmaids entertained, and the hour flew by in a flash of sandy feet and smiles. Even Sarah thawed enough to look acceptably happy in the photos.

As we headed back down the beach toward the surf club, a golden retriever ran out of the water. A suspiciously familiar golden retriever. Oh, no. My heart sank as Rufus loped along the sand towards us. He belonged to my neighbour, Mrs Johnson, and she let him roam the neighbourhood at will. I strode out ahead to meet him, hoping to head him off.

He ran toward me, tongue lolling happily out of his mouth.

"Go home, Rufus," I whispered at him, but he was in a playful mood and circled around me, wet tail wagging, heading straight for the bridal party. The little flower girls squealed and ducked behind the best man as Rufus bore down on the group.

"Go away, dog," Marco ordered, stepping half in front of Molly.

He probably knew what was coming, as did I, but there was nothing anyone could do to stop it. It was like watching a train wreck in slow motion as Rufus began to shake. From his black nose, down his head, through his shoulders and all down his long dripping body to the tip of his feathery tail, he shook, and water flew everywhere. Sandy, salty water.

Molly screamed as she and Marco took the full brunt of Rufus's efforts. I darted forward and grabbed his collar, trying to haul him away bodily. He thought that was a great game and leapt up to place his dirty, sandy paws on my clean T-shirt.

"Get down. Go home." I shoved him away, trying to protect my camera. There was no hope for my clothes.

"My dress!" Molly cried. "Look at it. It's ruined! Get that filthy mutt away from me!"

"Is that your dog?" Marco asked. If looks could have killed, I would have dropped dead right there on the sand.

"Never seen him before," I lied cheerfully, giving Rufus another shove. Thankfully, he got the message this time and headed off in the direction of the boat ramp and home.

"It's just water, Molly," Sarah said, brushing vigorously at her sister's dress. "Get a grip."

Just water—and half a beach's worth of sand. And maybe a sprinkling of outright dirt. The once-white dress was looking a little worse for wear.

"It's fine, honey," Marco said. "It will be dry by the time we get back to the surf club."

"See?" Sarah said, wiping sandy hands down the sides of her own blue dress. "There's hardly a mark now."

Molly sniffed, perilously close to tears.

"And if anything shows up in the photos," I added hastily, "I can just Photoshop it out."

"There you go—Charlie can Photoshop it out," Marco said, giving his bride an encouraging kiss. "Now, where's that beautiful smile gone?"

She gave him a watery smile and I breathed a sigh of relief. Of course I wanted her to have the wedding day she'd dreamed of, but I also had a lot on the line here. My photography business was brand-new, and I'd never photographed a wedding before. If this went well, I could expect a lot more business—and heaven knew, I needed it. Moving to Sunrise Bay from Sydney had been a spontaneous decision, and I certainly didn't regret it, but I'd left a good job behind and gone way, way out on a limb here.

And I was the least spontaneous person I knew. This wedding was hugely important to my fledgling business. Nothing else could go wrong.

Famous last words.

CHAPTER 2

I TOOK TEN MINUTES AFTER THE ENTRY OF THE BRIDAL PARTY TO gulp down my dinner, which I did standing in a corner of the kitchen, plate in hand. I was trying to stay out of everyone's way as the chefs were all bustling around plating up meals and putting last-minute touches to them before they went out the door.

"This chicken is still pink inside," the head chef snarled, brandishing a piece of chicken breast on a fork in the face of the under-chef who was in charge of tonight's chicken dish. "We don't want it clucking when the guests cut into it."

I tucked myself further into the corner, feeling sorry for the under-chef, who was wilting under the chef's criticism.

"But the chicken should be moist," the young chef protested.

"Moist, yes," the chef growled. "Undercooked, no. Look at this colour! Do you want half the guests to go home with salmonella poisoning? Do you want the *Sunny Bay Star* to be full of reports about the dangers of eating at the surf club?" His voice rose with each question, until he looked as though he wished his fork were a club he could use on the young chef. *"Do you want to be looking for a new job next week?"*

"No, chef."

The chef slammed the offending piece of chicken back on the grill. "Then make sure this chicken is cooked through before you serve it to anyone. Do I have to check every piece to make sure you've done your job?"

"No, chef," the under-chef repeated. The poor guy's face was as pink as the offending chicken. "I'll make sure they're cooked through."

"Good. See that you do."

I felt bad that a dozen people, including me, had witnessed him being told off like a little kid. I hadn't realised before what a high-pressure job cooking could be. But I was still glad that I was chowing down on the beef option. Salmonella poisoning was no fun.

Three of the wait staff were huddled at the doors into the venue, waiting to take the first plates out. One of them, a girl about my age with platinum-blond hair and a chest that strained the buttons on her white shirt, was smiling cajolingly up at the tall waiter next to her. He looked about nineteen, in that gawky stage where he hadn't started to fill out yet, and his black trousers didn't quite cover his ankles.

"Swap with me, Jimmy? I'll take table five and you take table ten."

"What's wrong with table ten?"

"My ex is sitting there."

"So? Two of mine are here."

"But we only broke up two weeks ago!" I felt sorry for her until she added, "And his wife is here, too. They just fired me. That's why I'm waitressing now."

"I don't know," Jimmy said, casting a doubtful look at an older woman in a waitress uniform who'd moved in to speak to the head chef. "Janice told me to do the tables on the left-hand side of the room."

"I'm sure she wouldn't care if we swap," the blond girl said. "*Please*, Jimmy. It's so awkward for me. Being in the same room is bad enough, but having to actually serve them dinner ... I don't think I can do it. That woman hates me. I don't want her to cause a scene. You don't want that either, do you, Jimmy? You wouldn't want the whole wedding to be ruined just because you wouldn't swap with me."

"I guess not," Jimmy said.

She smiled happily and patted his arm. Poor Jimmy never stood a chance. The blond girl sure knew how to manipulate a guy's feelings.

Suddenly the bustle in the kitchen rose to new heights, and more waiters appeared from nowhere. Dinner was ready to go out. Hastily, I ate the last few morsels of beef on my plate, scraping up as much of the red wine sauce as I could.

"Dinner was delicious," I said to the chef. "Thank you."

"You're welcome," he said, looking up with a

distracted smile. "Come back later. I'll save a dessert for you, too."

There must have been a hundred people in the function room of the surf club. I'd never before thought about the effort required to get a hundred dinners ready at virtually the same time. It was a big job and required a great deal of coordination. I grabbed my camera and headed through the swinging doors with the first of the waiters. Time to get back to my own job.

The function room wasn't the best-looking venue I'd ever seen—the carpet was a bit tired, and the seats were only molded plastic. But any deficiencies in the room were more than made up for by having the most glorious views of the ocean through the glass walls on the eastern side. There was nothing but sand and sea outside, and the long sweep of Sunrise Bay beach curling around to the distant headland.

Inside, each round table was covered in a crisp, white cloth, and a basket of pale pink flowers decorated the centre. Blue bows the same colour as the bridesmaids' dresses were tied around the back of each chair. The DJ next to the tiny dance floor was playing soft dinner music that involved a lot of pan flutes and chiming bells, which the buzz of conversation all but drowned out.

I started working my way around the room, taking photos of each table. There were only ten, so I hadn't thought it would take long, but I had to ask some people to leave their places and stand behind others, so I had all the guests grouped on the same side of the table for the shot. It was astonishing how long that took. You would have thought I was asking people to pack for a world trip. Inevitably one person would hold up the whole group by insisting they needed to reapply their lipstick, or they had to check a mirror to make sure there was nothing caught in their teeth.

Priya was seated next to Troy, since Sarah was at the bridal table. She hopped out of her seat with alacrity when I got to her table and lined up behind the guests on the other side for the photo.

"How's Troy?" I asked quietly once the photos were done and the guests were resettling themselves.

"Terrible company. My cat is a better conversationalist. He's spent the last half hour drinking beer and glowering at Ben Cassar."

"That's the guy he took a swing at?" When she nodded, I added, "What's his beef with him?"

"Search me. But don't worry, your intrepid reporter will have the story by the end of the night. I bet it's juicy, too. Sarah's already been over begging him to stop drinking and go home."

I glanced at Troy, who had resumed his seat and was staring moodily into his beer. "Looks like you've got a fun night ahead."

"Not to worry. It couldn't be worse than the last wedding I went to. They seated me at the kids' table."

"Were you a kid?"

She sidestepped a waiter who was squeezing past with an armful of dinners and grimaced. "It was last year."

She took her seat again and I moved on to the next table. I'd learned from my mistakes with the first couple of tables, and I was faster with this one, even though the waiters were dropping off meals as I was directing people where to stand. Though I'd just eaten, my stomach rumbled as the delicious smells wafted past me. That chicken looked just as good as the beef had been. The under-chef's job should be safe for another night.

Some of the more expensive Sydney venues were offering wedding packages where the guests could nominate ahead of time which meal they would like, but Sunny Bay wasn't that modern—or pricy. If you were a vegetarian or had food intolerances, most places would accommodate you, but everyone else had to take what they were given, the dishes alternating around the table. If you didn't like the option you ended up with, you just had to hope your neighbour agreed to a swap. Fortunately, in this case, both options looked and smelled great.

I tried not to get in the waiters' way, but there was only so much room between tables, and we ended up jostling each other as well as the guests who were trying to line up for the photo. Jimmy, the tall young waiter who had swapped with the blonde, almost dropped one of his plates into a guest's lap, but he recovered before the guest realised their peril. It seemed as though there were people everywhere for a moment, but the waiters had obviously done this a time or two before. They wove in and out in pairs, plonking down their plates in alternating order: chicken, beef, chicken, beef, as if it were a dance.

In only a moment, they had moved on to the next table.

The food was a distraction, and it took me another five minutes to get everyone posed for the photo.

"Right!" I said cheerfully at last. "Is everyone ready? Looking this way, please ... and ... smile." Ben Cassar was at this table, and he looked away just before I pressed the shutter. There was always one! I followed his gaze and saw the blond waitress on the other side of the room. Admittedly, that tight shirt of hers was fairly eye-catching, but he seemed more interested in the waitress than a man sitting next to his wife ought to be. "Sir? Could you look this way? And can everyone scrunch in a little closer?"

The standing guests squashed up a little more, and the seated people shuffled their chairs closer. Ben tugged his wife's chair closer, then put his arm around her. She shrugged it off, leaning a little away from him. Maybe she'd seen him checking out the waitress.

On Ben's other side was a little old man who was so hunched over he was no bigger than a ten-year-old. He wore a tweed jacket and a snazzy red bowtie. His hair was almost non-existent, but what there was stood out in a fluffy white cloud around his ears. Maybe his teeth were false, but his smile was bright.

"Is this my best angle?" he asked, grinning hugely at me as he turned his head slowly to the camera. I could practically hear his neck creaking.

"Perfect," I said. "Hold that pose for me!"

I took lots more shots, clicking away with gay abandon. One thing that every photographer learned early on was how hard it was to take photos of groups. There was always someone with their eyes shut or pulling a weird face. The bald guy next to the cute little old man acted as if smiling cost him money, and in the end I had to settle for "less grumpy". Thankfully, in the digital age we didn't have to pay to develop a dozen shots where Aunt Betty had screwed up her face or Uncle Dennis looked half-sozzled before we found one where everyone looked half-decent. And when all else failed, there was always Photoshop.

It wasn't until I was finished that I noticed the sign on its little stand next to the flower arrangement in the middle of the table. This was table ten.

"Thanks, everyone." Now Ben Cassar's roving eye made sense. I bet he was the ex-boss the blond waitress had been having the affair with. The way his wife had shrugged his arm away suggested he was in deep marital doo-doo. "Enjoy your dinner!"

CHAPTER 3

I MOVED ON TO THE NEXT TABLE, WHERE THE CLINK OF CUTLERY had replaced conversation as everyone tucked into their meals. My friend Andrea was seated there, looking far more glamorous than I'd ever seen her. She usually wore jeans and button-up shirts for her job at the library, but tonight she'd gone all-out with a red dress that clung to her curves and showed enough cleavage that it was a wonder Ben Cassar wasn't staring.

A man took the seat next to her as I approached, and she introduced him as her date, Nick Kettlewell.

"How do you find the Canon?" he asked. "I like a Nikon myself."

"It's great. Got all the features I need, plus a beautiful range of lenses. Are you interested in photography?"

"Not as much these days, but I used to dabble when I was younger. I did Photography at school and I even had my own darkroom for a while." He grinned. "I was a terrible snob about film in those days. I always said I'd never go digital, but ..." He spread his hands in a helpless gesture.

"Admittedly the first digital cameras weren't anywhere near as high quality as film," I said, "so maybe you were right to be snobby. But for a job like this, it's so helpful to be able to see the shot straight away."

"Oh, don't worry, I'm a convert now. You can't beat the convenience of digital."

We continued chatting until a burst of masculine laughter from the next table interrupted us. I glanced over and saw Marco's boss the centre of attention.

"You know that guy?" I asked Andrea. I was dying to know if she could shed any light on why Troy had attacked him. "Sarah and Troy don't seem too happy that he's here."

"Sure," Andrea said, following my gaze. "Who doesn't? That's Ben Cassar, pillar of the community—if you believe his PR."

"And if you don't?"

"Take your pick," Nick said with a scowl. "Dodgy businessman, thieving scum. Absolute piece of—"

"I see you don't like him either."

"To know him is to hate him."

"You forgot *unfaithful husband*," Andrea said.

"He's having an affair?" That confirmed my guess that he was the blonde's ex-boss.

"*An* affair?" Andrea laughed and Nick snorted, shaking his head. "He must have had a dozen over the years. I don't know why Gail puts up with him."

"Because he makes a lot of money," Nick said. "It's definitely not for his personality."

"Probably," she said. "Although if it were me, I'd divorce him and take as much of that money for myself as I could. Still, it takes all sorts to make a world, doesn't it? Maybe she really loves him, deep down."

"It would have to be pretty deep down," I said, remembering the way Gail had shrugged off his arm and moved as far away from him as she could for the group photo. Even the feathers of her hat had bobbed as if trying to shoo him away. "She doesn't seem to like him all that much at the moment, much less love him."

"That would be because she's just found out about his latest affair, I'm guessing. Cynthia told me a couple of weeks ago that he's been getting it on with his receptionist."

"Such a cliché," Nick said. "And so typical of Ben."

"Gail demanded he sack the girl and he's been trying to crawl back into her good graces ever since." Andrea glanced over at the next table. "It's probably going to take him a while. Apparently the receptionist was very pretty."

I nodded, thinking of the blond waitress. It must be her, unless there were *two* cheating husbands at table ten, which didn't seem likely.

Cheating on one's partner was a pretty sore subject for me lately, considering it wasn't all that long since I had come home to find my fiancé in bed with my best friend. I should have been knee deep in last-minute wedding preparations and celebrations right now. Instead, I'd cancelled my wedding, left my job, and moved out of

Sydney to start a new life here in Sunrise Bay. Or, as we locals liked to call it, Sunny Bay. It was such a welcoming place that I felt like a local already.

I glared at the back of Ben Cassar's dark head. Bad enough to betray a fiancé, the way Will had done to me, but this Ben guy was married. He'd already promised to love, honour, and cherish, and to remain faithful for the rest of his life. It was depressing how fast some people could go from heartfelt vows such as we had all witnessed this afternoon on the beach to messing around with the receptionist.

On Andrea's other side was an empty seat with a pink cardigan thrown over the back and a half-finished chicken dinner on the table in front of it.

"Are we missing someone here?" I asked her.

"Jo's just gone to the bathroom," she said. "In rather a hurry, actually."

Oh, dear. I eyed the chicken suspiciously, but there wasn't a trace of pink in its creamy white flesh.

"I'll come back later," I said.

A bathroom break wasn't a bad idea, come to think of it. Once the speeches began I'd be busy for a while. I headed in the direction of the ladies' room.

I went in and found a cramped room with only three cubicles. Coming out of one of them was the lady in the pink straw hat who'd cried such floods of tears at the wedding. She didn't look much better now. Her eyes were still red and her face was unnaturally pale. In fact, she looked unwell, and thoughts of undercooked chicken and salmonella poisoning leapt into my mind again.

"Lovely wedding, isn't it?" I said and she jumped, as if she'd been lost in her own thoughts and hadn't expected me to speak.

Her red-rimmed eyes met mine. "Lovely. You're the photographer?"

"Yes." It hadn't required much deductive reasoning on her part, considering I had a camera with a honking great lens on it hanging around my neck. "I love your hat."

"Thanks." She moved to the basins to wash her hands and I headed into one of the cubicles.

When I came back to Andrea's table, pink hat lady was there, sitting next to my friend. So she was the missing Jo.

"If I could interrupt you for just a moment, ladies and gentlemen," I began, then launched into my usual patter. Most of them were already finished their meals.

I soon had them arranged in a pleasant grouping, though I had to ask Jo to swap seats with the gentleman next to her, as her outsized hat was blocking part of Andrea's face. I clicked away, conscious of the time, then moved on to the next table, giving Andrea a little wave goodbye.

By the time I had visited each table the MC was on his feet, microphone in hand. "Ladies and gentlemen, I hope you've all enjoyed your main course. The lovely staff here at the Sunny Bay Surf Club will be bringing out your desserts soon, and while they're doing that, it's time to hear a few words from the man of the hour, Marco Lombardi."

Everyone clapped as Marco got to his feet, pulling a folded sheet of paper from his breast pocket. He stepped up to the microphone and cleared his throat nervously. "On behalf of my wife and I ..." He stopped as everyone started clapping again, and a broad smile lit his face. "*My wife and I.* I like the way that sounds."

He went on to thank the bridesmaids for their support of the bride. *Thanks?* Those poor women deserved a *medal* for putting up with Molly's tantrums. Then he thanked both sets of parents. In fact, he was grateful to a whole long list of people, and I stopped listening after a while. In my head I was going over the list of "must-have" shots I still needed to take: cutting the cake, the first dance, tossing the bouquet and the garter—if Molly was wearing one—and the farewells. That should cover it. Plus of course a few of each speaker and some nice reaction shots from the bride and groom. I was snapping away as I thought.

The two little flowergirls grew bored during the speeches and slipped from their seats. They weren't sitting with the bridal party at the bridal table but with their parents. They started a game of hide and seek behind the columns at the back of the room that supported big urns full of flowers. They looked so cute that I took a few shots of them, flower crowns askew and mischievous grins lighting their faces, before their mother hustled them back to their seats.

The last speech was finished and the final toast was drunk and I eyed the desserts rather longingly. Chocolate mud cake or pavlova—both looked equally delicious. I hoped the head chef had kept his promise to save me something. I noticed that Molly and Marco hadn't even touched theirs. Perhaps they were too nervous, or too distracted by their guests. Or maybe Molly had given herself indigestion with her bad temper.

Cutting the cake was up next. Molly and Marco left their seats and approached the wedding cake, which was three tiers of frothing flowers over acres of white icing. It was the biggest wedding cake I'd ever seen. Everyone in the room could have three slices and there'd still be plenty left over.

One of the waiters brought out an enormous knife with a white ribbon around its handle, which Molly took. Marco put his hand over hers and they inserted the blade into the bottom layer.

"Looking this way," I said, and they smiled at me. The smiles were a little strained by this point. Their faces probably ached from all the smiling they'd done tonight. Everyone clapped again and a couple of shrill whistles split the air as they gingerly sliced through the cake.

They were still standing there posing as a dozen relatives crowded around to take a similar photo when I heard a thud and a rattle of crockery. Someone shrieked and I spun around. A man was slumped in his seat, sprawled across the table in front of him. It was Marco's cheating boss, Ben. His wife, Gail, stood over him, feathers flapping in alarm, and several other people had leapt up and were crowding around too, including Priya.

"Someone call an ambulance," she said, her calm tones carrying over the rising jumble of voices. "I think he's having a heart attack."

CHAPTER 4

THE STAFF SWUNG INTO ACTION. UNDER THE DIRECTION OF ONE of the guests, who was a doctor, two waiters helped Ben Cassar from the room, presumably to rest somewhere less public until the ambulance arrived. He stumbled along between them, his face an awful grey. But surely he wouldn't have been able to walk if he were really having a heart attack? I hoped Priya was wrong. Maybe the blame could be laid at the chicken's door. The under-chef's job prospects were looking dicey again.

Molly looked furious at such drama in the middle of her reception—at least, drama that she didn't cause herself. Everyone milled around for a while, unsure what to do. Eventually, the MC took back the microphone to report that the ambulance had arrived and Ben was on his way to the hospital. He told a few jokes and the guests relaxed, comfortable that the patient was in expert hands.

I didn't have much time to think about it, since it was soon time for the bridal waltz and I was busy for a while getting photos of all the important players. My favourites were the ones of Molly dancing with her dad, who beamed down at her with such obvious pride that it almost made me forgive her for being such a bridezilla. Almost. But it was still a lovely moment, and I was sure it was a photo that her dad would treasure, even if Molly didn't.

I prowled the edges of the dance floor, getting lots of candid shots. I wanted to make sure that Molly and Marco were happy, since I was relying on their testimonials on my website—hopefully glowing!—to get me more business. The overhead lights had been dimmed for the dancing, and coloured lights swept the dance floor instead. These photos should be a lot of fun.

A couple of hours later, I stole a moment to sit down next to Andrea, who was alone at her table. Finally I was almost done.

"You're not dancing? Where's Nick?"

"Gone off to talk to one of Molly's cousins." She nodded at the next table, where Nick was deep in conversation with the surly-looking guy who'd been sitting next to the cute little old man. His old-fashioned jacket suggested he didn't wear formal attire too often. "They went to school together but they don't get a chance to catch up often."

"Does everyone in this town know everyone else?"

"Pretty much. Give it a few years and you'll know everyone, too."

"So ... Nick." I lifted an eyebrow and waited to see what my friend would say.

Andrea grinned. "He's just a guy I met at the gym. He's

a carpenter by trade, but he doesn't have much work now because he refuses to work with Cassar's company, and they're the biggest game in town. We have coffee together sometimes after a workout."

"And now you're going out? Whatever would Mr Darcy say?" Our book club had read *Pride and Prejudice* recently, and Andrea was a huge fan of the book's hero.

She laughed. "I can hardly invite Mr Darcy to be my date for a wedding. He's only my book boyfriend."

"Whereas Nick is your real-life boyfriend?" Aunt Evie had told me that Andrea had never been out with the same guy more than once since her divorce. If she and Nick were meeting for coffee and now she had invited him to this wedding, things were looking up.

"Don't jump to any conclusions! He's not my boyfriend. I just needed a date for tonight. There's nothing worse than going to a wedding on your own and being stuck on the table with all the elderly spinsters and that one guy from the bride's work who couldn't get a date to save his life. I didn't want to get set up with anyone. They put Eric Harding next to poor Jo because she came alone, and she had to listen to him bang on about football all night."

"Is Jo all right? She didn't look too good when I saw her in the bathroom earlier."

"She told me her husband died last year. Weddings must be hard for her."

"Oh, no! Poor thing. No wonder she cried so much at the ceremony. It must have brought back all sorts of memories."

"Yeah. If it were me, I wouldn't have come. Especially if I knew I'd end up sitting next to Eric Harding."

"Maybe she should have brought a friend. They might have been able to cheer her up." I looked across the dance floor at all the people enjoying themselves. You never knew what life had in store for you next. "Well, your date seems nice. And you didn't get stuck with Eric Harding. But hey, it could have been worse. You could have been at the table with the guy who had the heart attack."

She rolled her eyes. "Actually, we were meant to be. You should have seen Nick's face when he saw the seating plan. I thought he was going to head straight back to the car for a minute. Luckily another couple agreed to swap with us."

"He must really dislike Ben Cassar."

"He hates the guy. Can't stand him. Fortunately I've managed to keep him distracted with my sparkling repartee and a handy bottle of wine. I think he's had a pretty good night."

I laughed. "That's good. I think everyone has enjoyed it—except for Ben Cassar, I guess. I hope he's okay."

"I'm sure we would have heard something if he wasn't."

"And maybe Troy didn't have a super great night either." I looked around and spotted him out on the balcony with Sarah and another couple, laughing and chatting. His mood must have improved once Ben Cassar left.

"At least all the drama doesn't seem to have spoiled

Molly and Marco's night. They've only had eyes for each other."

"True." I looked around. The last I had seen of the newlyweds, they'd been cuddled up together on the dance floor, but now there was no sign of them. Sudden panic spiked through me. Had I missed something? "Where are they?"

Andrea checked her watch. "It's ten-thirty so they've probably gone to get changed. I think the surf club will be throwing us out soon."

Sure enough, the DJ stopped the music and the lights came back on full. I blinked a couple of times at the sudden brightness. Somehow it made me feel even more tired than I had before.

"If we could have all the single ladies up here on the dance floor," the DJ said, "it's time for the bride to throw her bouquet."

Amid much giggling, women gathered on the dance floor. One of the bridesmaids was there and several others who looked as though they had been enjoying the free alcohol just a little too much. Andrea hadn't moved from her seat.

"Get up there," I said, rising from my own chair since duty called again. "You're single."

Andrea gave me a lazy smile. "Single and loving it. You wouldn't get me up there if the building were on fire. Besides, I'm too old and crusty. Let the young ones have their fun."

I laughed. "Yes, Grandma. Shall I bring you your false teeth, too?"

"Get up there yourself. You're single."

"Ah, but I'm working." I waved my camera at her and headed for the dance floor just as Molly and Marco came back into the room. They had removed their wedding finery, and now Molly wore a pink form-fitting dress that had a slit up the side that was almost indecent. She was carrying a bouquet of pale pink roses that was much smaller than her bridal bouquet. Marco had on a white shirt and a tie in the same pink.

With some prodding from the DJ the single ladies formed a tight, expectant crowd. Molly turned her back to them, then launched the bouquet over her head. Several of the women screamed and there was a bit of push and shove but Priya emerged from the scrum triumphant, waving the bouquet above her head like a trophy. I caught the expression of delight on her face perfectly. I even had a shot of the flowers suspended in mid-air, hovering above a sea of raised hands, just before she caught it.

"Okay, fellas," the DJ said when the noise and laughter had died down. "It's your turn now. Can I have all the single gents on the dance floor, please."

Nick didn't share Andrea's reticence. He joined the growing group in front of the DJ and elbowed his way to the front.

One of the staff brought out a chair and Molly put one foot up on it. To laughter and shouts of encouragement from the gathered men, Marco slid the garter down her leg.

When he threw it, the men proved to be even more competitive than the women had been. A couple of them hit the floor in the tussle. But the victor was Nick, a huge grin on his face. I glanced back at Andrea and she was shaking her head, smiling. She'd get a lot more questions, now.

After that I was kept busy as the DJ got everyone arranged in a big circle to say goodbye. Marco and Molly went around the circle kissing and hugging their guests and I got some great shots. It probably took twenty minutes, but since I was busy the time seemed to fly. Before I knew it, the crowd was streaming outside to wave goodbye. Molly and Marco hopped into the waiting limo and drove away with a last wave. As the limo left the car park, a police car pulled in.

I found Andrea at my elbow. "Thank goodness that's over. My feet are killing me."

She had on a pair of shoes with the wickedest heels I had ever seen. "No wonder you look tall tonight."

Nick was still talking to Molly's cousin. The man seemed more relaxed now, even laughing at something Nick had said as he finished his cigarette. Nick joined us when the man went back inside.

"I haven't spoken to Larry in years," he said to Andrea. "Probably not since we left school."

"Was he in your year?" I asked doubtfully. That guy had looked a lot older than Nick.

"In my year?" Nick laughed. "He was in all my classes, except for Maths. We practically lived in each other's pockets."

"You've certainly aged better than he has," Andrea purred.

The sound of slamming car doors drew my attention. Two police officers had gotten out of the patrol car—my favourite two police officers, Curtis Kane and Delia Backhouse.

And wow, what kind of life was I living where I had favourite police officers? We sure weren't in Kansas anymore, Toto.

"What's your boyfriend doing here?" Andrea asked, frowning as they walked briskly across the car park towards the entrance of the surf club.

I felt a blush heating my cheeks. Thank goodness it was dark out here. "He's not my boyfriend! I hardly know the guy."

Andrea looked at me with amusement. "But you'd like to know him better."

"My personal life is way too messed up at the moment to even *think* about dating anyone."

Which was a hundred per cent true—but I might juuust possibly have considered the idea once or twice. Okay, maybe three times. Or seventeen. But hey, was it my fault the man had biceps the size of my head and a dimple that made me weak at the knees when he smiled? I would have to be *dead* not to notice how attractive he was. It didn't mean I was going to do anything about it.

Priya exchanged a smiling glance with Andrea as she joined us. "Whatever you say."

"Hey, *you're* the one who caught the bouquet," I said. "Let's talk about *your* romantic prospects, shall we?"

But she wasn't listening, her attention caught as Delia

waved her arms and shouted, "Ladies and gentlemen, could we all go back inside, please?"

Delia had her cool, professional face on, her short hair tucked away under her uniform hat. I knew she was my height, but she looked tiny next to Curtis, who was well over six foot and built like a professional footballer. He loomed next to her, his face serious.

"What's going on?" someone called.

"We've been sent to secure the scene," she replied, radiating calm authority. "I'm afraid Mr Cassar has been murdered."

CHAPTER 5

A<small>T LEAST HALF THE GUESTS HAD ALREADY LEFT</small>, <small>BUT EVERYONE</small> else trooped back inside in a buzz of excited conversation.

"We'll try not to keep you too long," Curtis said, directing everyone to one end of the room. "We'll get some initial statements and then send you on your way."

Two more police came in, followed by two men in plain clothes I assumed were detectives.

"How do they know it's a murder?" Priya asked, her eyes scanning the crowd. "I thought the guy had a heart attack?"

"Are they sure it wasn't food poisoning?" Andrea added, starting a whisper among a nearby group as to who had had the chicken.

Thinking about food reminded me that the chef had promised to save me a dessert. I hoped he'd picked the chocolate one. I liked pavlova, too, but that chocolate mud cake had looked amazing. If we were going to be here for a while I might as well eat.

I slipped away and opened the swinging double doors to the kitchen. Delia was in there, poking around in the bins, watched anxiously by the head chef, a couple of waiters, and the kitchen staff.

"As you can see," the chef said, gesturing at the industrial dishwasher whirring away on one side of the room, "if there was any evidence, it's all been washed away by now."

"What about food scraps?" she asked.

"All disposed of. Together, in one big bin. Will you test the whole lot?"

Delia sighed and turned to the waiters. "I know you're all wanting to get home, so I'll be as quick as I can. Who here served Ben Cassar tonight?" She consulted the seating plan in her hand. "He was on table ten."

Jimmy, the tall young man who'd replaced the blond waitress, put up his hand like the schoolboy he'd obviously so recently been. "That would be me."

"And me," one of the others said.

At that moment, the blonde entered the kitchen, wiping damp hands on her black apron. She stopped in surprise at finding a police officer in the middle of the room and glanced at me. "What's this all about?"

Had she been in the bathroom and missed the announcement? Oh, dear.

"There's been a murder," Jimmy said.

Her gaze locked onto Delia's face. "Who?"

"Ben Cassar."

"No." She looked around the room, her eyes pleading. "No."

But every face was serious, and I could see the moment she accepted that Delia wasn't lying. Her face crumpled. Her eyes closed and her mouth opened, and a scream of primal anguish came out.

"Oh, Ella, honey." An older waitress put her arms around her, and Ella collapsed against her, sobbing.

In the end she had to be led away by the woman before Delia could continue. Not that there was much more for Delia to do. Neither Jimmy nor the other waiter who'd served table ten had seen anything untoward. All the plates had looked the same, all the bottles of wine had been delivered unopened to the table. She went back into the function room and I followed her out, all desire for chocolate cake gone in the face of such grief.

What a way to end a wedding. At least Molly and Marco had already left.

"What about the other guests?" I asked her. "The ones who'd already left before you got here? One of them might have seen something."

"We'll get to them tomorrow and in the next few days," she said. "Murder investigations take time. Nothing will be solved tonight."

The police had been busy while I'd been in the kitchen. Two investigators were inspecting table ten, though what they hoped to find I couldn't imagine. From Delia's questions in the kitchen, it seemed that Ben Cassar had been poisoned, but table ten only had a couple of empty coffee cups remaining on it, plus the flower arrangement and assorted place cards. The waiters had cleared everything else away.

The remaining guests had been corralled at one end of the room, and the two homicide detectives, plus Curtis and another two officers, were busy taking statements. I imagined they were going just as well as the interviews in the kitchen had—no one had been paying particular attention to Ben Cassar until the moment he collapsed. What was there to say? I bet they were hearing a lot of *I saw nothing.*

Probably the only person happy with the investigation so far would be the head chef, since we clearly weren't talking about salmonella poisoning. No need to fear that undercooked chicken would be garnering bad reviews in the local paper.

A policeman directed me to wait with the group that the older detective was interviewing. This included the DJ and the remaining people from Ben Cassar's table. No one was talking as they waited their turn, some looking sombre, others just tired and clearly impatient to leave.

The other detective was on the far side of the room talking to Troy. Interviewees came and went from the other tables, but Troy still sat there. I wished I could hear what they were saying, but they were too far away and there was too much other noise in the big room. Troy was sitting with his arms folded defensively, a sullen look on his face. Sarah was watching them, too, from her place among the other guests, her hands clenched together tightly in her lap.

My turn came, and the detective gestured wordlessly at the chair beside him. He was seated at the table closest to the bridal table, and there was still a half-eaten piece of wedding cake discarded at his elbow. His greying hair was rumpled, as if he'd been woken up and hadn't bothered brushing his hair, just thrown on his black pants and ugly checked shirt before heading out the door. I felt a momentary twinge of sympathy at the hours his job forced on him.

"I'm Detective McGovern. And you are?" His pen was poised over his notepad and he didn't even look up. Somebody was grumpy about being called out in the middle of the night.

"Charlie Carter. *Charlotte* Carter." Did he need my full name? I'd been interviewed by the police before—by Curtis, in fact, but I couldn't remember. Curtis had been much warmer than Detective McGovern. He hadn't even laughed at me when I couldn't remember my own address. In my defence, I'd only just moved in.

"You're the photographer?

"Yes."

"Did you know Ben Cassar?"

"No."

"Did you see anyone touch his food or drink tonight?"

"No. So he was poisoned?"

That made him look up, but only to scowl at me. "I'll ask the questions, thank you, Miss Carter."

I had the feeling that I wouldn't be adding Detective McGovern to my list of favourite police officers.

"See anyone acting suspiciously around him?" he continued.

"No."

He sighed and offered me a business card from a small

stack on the table in front of him. "Thank you, Miss Carter. If you think of anything else, please ring me on that number."

As I took it, a policeman came over and murmured something in Detective McGovern's ear. Something that made him sit up straight, all signs of tiredness gone.

"Show me."

The policeman handed over a small black bag with a long strap—not a ladies' handbag, more like something you would use for travel, plain and serviceable, though no bigger than a small purse. Detective McGovern put on a pair of disposable gloves, unzipped it, glanced inside, then strode over to the table where his partner was still interviewing Troy.

"Is this yours?" he demanded.

"Yes," Troy said. "It's my—"

"You want to explain to me why you brought needles to a wedding?" He pulled out a syringe and brandished it in Troy's face.

"Because I'm a diabetic. I take needles and insulin with me everywhere."

The two detectives exchanged a glance.

"That's very convenient."

"There's nothing *convenient* about diabetes, mate," Troy growled, his face reddening.

"We'll have to continue this conversation at the station," Detective McGovern said.

"Why? I've told you, I've got diabetes. I haven't done anything wrong." Troy stood up, fists clenched.

McGovern's partner stood up, too, and the room stilled, everyone anticipating violence.

"You can come to the station with us of your own accord," McGovern said evenly, "or we can arrest you. Your choice. *Mate*."

CHAPTER 6

I arrived home at one o'clock on Sunday morning and fell straight into bed, worn out from the drama of the past few hours, on top of the stress of actually photographing my first wedding. I didn't surface again until midday, and spent the afternoon going through the photos from the wedding, cropping and correcting them, then uploading them to the wedding gallery on my website. I'd been dying to see how they turned out and, on the whole, I was pretty happy with my work.

It seemed more likely to me that the murderer would have been one of the guests at the wedding than one of the waiters or kitchen staff. I spent a long time staring at the group photo of table ten, wondering if one of those smiling faces belonged to a murderer.

Or, perhaps more likely, one of those unsmiling faces —Ben's wife was right beside him, looking as though it physically pained her to sit next to him. And then there was Larry, that surly-looking friend of Nick's, acting like the whole wedding had been put on for the express purpose of annoying him. He was a big lump of a man, and his sour expression made him look like the kind of guy that wouldn't think twice about offing someone at dinner.

I wondered how Troy and Sarah were doing, and how Troy's interview at the police station had gone. Clearly Detective McGovern thought that Troy had somehow injected Cassar with poison, probably during their fight. I sent Sarah a text, not meaning to be nosy, just wanting to let her know I was thinking of her. It seemed the friendly thing to do. But she never replied.

On Monday morning, the doorbell rang as I finished washing up my breakfast things. I looked at the clock and my heart sank. 9:15. Again.

"Good morning," Steve said when I opened the door. He was the local florist's husband and made all her deliveries for her. I was getting to know Steve quite well lately. Today he had a bunch of cheery yellow roses for me.

"Denise thought you might like a change of colour after all those red ones." He held the roses out to me but I didn't take them. They were beautiful, buds just beginning to open and mixed with deep green foliage and some dainty white baby's breath. It was all presented with Denise's usual flair, wrapped in soft lavender paper tied with a yellow ribbon.

"Can't you give them to someone else? The nursing home or the hospital, maybe?"

He shook his head, a disappointed look on his face. I immediately felt bad for rejecting Denise's lovely roses. My rejection had nothing to do with the flowers themselves. "Your boyfriend paid for them, so we have to deliver them where he wants them to be delivered. Don't you like them?"

I sighed. "Will is not my boyfriend. Not anymore. And the roses are beautiful, but I don't want to accept any more flowers from him. I'm only going to give them away just like all the others."

He pushed the bunch towards me. "That's your prerogative, of course. They're your roses so you can do whatever you like with them. All I have to do is deliver them."

I took them reluctantly and he headed off with a cheery, "See you tomorrow!"

I hoped he wouldn't, but I had a bad feeling about that. I knew perfectly well how stubborn Will could be when he set his mind to something. And apparently, for reasons of his own, he'd set his mind to winning me back.

I heard Mrs Johnson's front door open in the duplex next door, followed by the scrape of doggy nails on her driveway. Rufus pushed through the line of low bushes that separated our driveways, his tongue lolling out in a happy doggy smile. He'd come through there so often lately that he was wearing a track through the garden, and the bushes in question were looking rather forlorn.

"Hey there, boy!" I shifted the bunch of flowers to one arm and leaned down to pat him with the other. He wagged happily at the attention.

"Hello, dear," Mrs Johnson said, stepping out her front door. "No wonder Rufus was whining to go out. He must have heard your voice outside. I think he likes you more than me."

I laughed, stroking Rufus's soft head. He was a beautiful sandy colour that matched the golden sands of Sunrise Bay beach almost perfectly. His chocolate-brown eyes closed in pure delight as I caressed his velvety ears.

"I'm sure that's not true, Mrs Johnson. You're the one that feeds him, after all." Retrievers were notorious for their love of food. I was positive that the way to Rufus's heart was straight through his stomach.

"Yes, but I'm not a dog person." She wandered over, stopping just the other side of the bushes. Even though she was a tiny slip of a woman, they only came up to her waist. She reminded me a little of Aunt Evie, though she looked a good ten years older. Definitely the far side of eighty. Her white hair framed her face in soft curls and her blue eyes smiled behind large-framed glasses. "He was Bert's dog. I would have gotten rid of him after Bert died, except I knew Bert would be so angry if I did." She eyed my flowers curiously. "More flowers? You must have a lot of admirers."

"Only one—my ex-fiancé. You want them?"

"Oh, no, I couldn't take your flowers, dear. Why don't you want them? And why is your *ex*-fiancé sending flowers to you?"

"That's a very good question. I texted him and asked him to stop but they keep coming, every day for the past two weeks."

"What did he say when you texted him?"

"I don't know. I refuse to read his texts."

Her eyes widened behind the glasses. "You have more self-control than me. I wouldn't be able to resist peeking at them. My, my. And you have no intention of taking him back? Your house must be full of flowers by now!"

"It's not, because I've given them all away. I don't want anything to do with him ever again. He's wasting his money, but he's a stubborn man." And he had a lot of money to waste.

"Perhaps he's just in love. Men in love do strange things sometimes." Her eyes gleamed as if at a happy memory, and I wondered what Bert had gotten up to when he was alive.

Rufus wandered off to sniff at a nearby bush and I leaned against the brick wall of my home. It was warm from the heat of the sun. "If he was so deeply in love with me, why did he sleep with my best friend?"

Mrs Johnson's mouth formed an O of surprise. "He slept with your best friend? Goodness me. Young people these days! No wonder you don't want his flowers."

Rufus left those bushes and wandered into the next-door neighbour's front yard to see if there were any good smells there.

"Rufus!" I called. Mrs Johnson let him go wherever he wanted, but it bothered me. What if he got hit by a car? Or someone called the pound to take him away?

"Don't worry, dear. He always comes back in his own time."

That was true, but I wondered if he was lonely. If Mrs Johnson wasn't a dog person, maybe he was wandering Sunrise Bay looking for affection.

"Would you like me to take him for a walk?" I'd shower him with love if he were mine. His visits were the highlights of my days.

"I'm sure he'd love that, but I don't want to impose on you," Mrs Johnson said.

"You wouldn't be. I was just about to walk into town anyway. Is there a lead I could use?"

"Oh, you don't need that," she said cheerfully. "Bert had him trained to walk off leash. I'm sure he'll remember how to walk at heel if you tell him to."

I regarded Rufus doubtfully, and he looked up from whatever he'd been sniffing and gazed back at me in mindless happiness. Emphasis on the *mindless*. He didn't strike me as a mental giant, and I wondered if he would still remember Bert's training. He certainly hadn't seemed that well trained when he'd accompanied me around the town before. He'd just come and gone as he pleased. The incident on the beach on Saturday came to mind, where he'd shaken his gross, wet self all over the bride.

"Okay, I'll just get my shoes on. Are you sure you won't take these flowers off my hands?" I held the bouquet out to her.

"Well, if you're sure you don't want them." She took the roses and inhaled their scent deeply. "Ah, lovely. I'll enjoy your fiancé's guilt roses, even if you don't."

I laughed. "Someone may as well get some benefit out of all this money he's spending." I waved goodbye, then ducked inside to pull on my shoes.

When I came outside again, Mrs Johnson had gone in

and Rufus was sitting in the middle of my driveway scratching.

"You okay there, buddy?" I asked. He cocked his head in my direction but kept scratching. "Do you have fleas?"

Surely not. I couldn't imagine Mrs Johnson putting up with that, but it probably didn't hurt to check.

He continued scratching as I checked him over. I couldn't see anything but it might be a good idea to get some flea treatment to be safe. I stopped at the bottom of the driveway and looked back at him. "You want to go for a walk, boy?"

His ears pricked up and he came trotting down the driveway, his feathery tail waving like a banner behind him. I laughed. "Oh, you know that word, do you? *Walk.* You want to go for a *walk*?"

He bounded around me and that crazy tail whacked me in the back of the knees. "Oh, you do! Let's go, then." I headed down the street toward the beach and he trotted along beside me, occasionally ranging out to check out a particularly good smell or to lift his leg on a telegraph pole.

I didn't walk along the beach, because I didn't want to deliver a soaking wet dog back to Mrs Johnson, but we walked on the grassy footpath next to Beach Road, which ran along the beachfront. It was elevated some ten feet above the sand at this point, and we had a nice view of the whole long sweep of the bay and the houses perched on the northern headland.

That was where the rich folk lived—and Aunt Evie in her comfy villa at Sunrise Lodge. Which reminded me, I was meeting her for lunch today. She'd been a great support to me since I'd moved in, and it was nice to be able to see her anytime I liked without having to drive all the way up from Sydney and making a big occasion of it. It had been years since I'd had a relative living so close by and it was a lovely feeling.

Sunny Bay was a small community. It had plenty of shops, but they were mostly aimed at the tourist trade. Either they sold souvenirs, clothes, or art, or they were places to eat. There was a whole strip of restaurants, in just about every flavour you could name, along Beach Road. But if you wanted more practical options like department stores and big supermarkets with all the trimmings you had to drive to nearby Waterloo Bay.

Even so, there were plenty of cars about. I called Rufus to heel as we got close to the shopping strip, afraid he might run out into the road. He took up a position on my left, sticking close to my leg.

"Good boy!" I'd had serious doubts that he would remember how to do it, but he was heeling like a champ. Of course, it might not last if he saw something more enticing, but it was a good start. Maybe I'd buy him some doggie treats from the tiny supermarket here.

First things first, though. "You wait here for me, boy," I told him when we reached the florist shop. "Sit, Rufus. Stay."

He sat down, thumping his tail against the pavement, and I went inside. Buckets of flowers covered the floor, and finished arrangements in baskets and vases stood on stands behind them. Pretty pots and knickknacks filled the shelves that lined the walls, and the whole place smelled divine.

"Good morning," Denise said, looking up from some paperwork. She wore a clean white apron and had her brown hair pulled back in a short ponytail. "How is Miss Popularity this morning?"

"Wishing she wasn't quite so popular—at least not with that guy."

Her smile changed to a look of commiseration. "Steve told me you weren't happy about the flowers. Such a shame."

"It is. It seems like such a waste. Are you sure you can't deliver them to someone else?"

"Who?"

"Anyone! I don't care. I just hate being reminded of him every day."

Denise put her pen down and leaned against the counter. "I wish I could help you, but I doubt I'd stay in business long if I started delivering flowers anywhere I wanted to. Your admirer is paying me, so I have to follow the customer's instructions—unless you wanted to get the police involved?"

"The police?"

"If he's bothering you that much, you could get a restraining order."

"It's not like that. I don't feel threatened. Just annoyed." Will wasn't a danger to me. I knew him well enough to be sure of that. I sighed. "Well, at least you're making money out of him. And my next-door neighbour seemed very pleased with the yellow roses this morning, so it's not all bad."

Denise's smile peeked out again. "They were pretty, weren't they? Do you have any preferences for tomorrow? His order only specifies roses, but I could throw something else in there for you to make it more bearable."

"No, thanks." I looked around at all the buckets of beautiful flowers waiting to be made into arrangements. There were some lovely ones, but I didn't want anything from Will. "There's nothing wrong with the roses themselves, and I'm only going to give them away, so don't waste your time."

Rufus chose that moment to wander in through the open door.

"Oh, no, boy! You can't come in here. I'm sorry," I said to Denise. "He was supposed to wait outside, but I guess his obedience training is a little rusty."

"That's all right. I don't mind." Rufus sniffed at a bucket of gerberas and then sneezed. We both laughed and he looked at us rather reproachfully. "That's Bert Johnson's old dog, isn't it?"

"Yes, it is. I'm living next door to Mrs Johnson now. Oh, you know that already." Of course she did. I was an idiot. She'd only been delivering flowers to that address for the last two weeks. "Mrs Johnson says she's not really a dog person, so I thought I'd take Rufus for a walk."

"He has such beautiful eyes." Denise came around the counter to pat him. "How can she resist him?"

"He's gorgeous," I agreed. "But I bet he sheds something fierce."

"Yes, he looks as though he could do with a good brush. He's still got bits of winter coat here, see?"

He *was* looking a bit neglected. I guess you couldn't expect a woman in her eighties to groom a big dog like him, especially if she wasn't all that fond of dogs in the first place. I'd have to see if the supermarket had any dog brushes or combs when I went to get the treats.

"So how was the big wedding on Saturday?" Denise asked, straightening up again. Rufus immediately began to scratch. Flea treatment! Mustn't forget that either.

I grinned, remembering all the beautiful shots I'd taken on the beach. "It went really well—oh, except for ..." I caught my bottom lip between my teeth, feeling bad. It hadn't gone at all well for Ben Cassar, and it seemed a little insensitive to rave about the wedding in view of that.

"Except for Ben Cassar dying, you mean?" Denise asked. "I heard all about that. What a scandal! Poisoned, I heard. By Troy Chapman, if the rumours are true. I heard he was at the police station for hours afterwards."

Poor Troy. "I think the rumours are jumping the gun a bit."

She raised an eyebrow. "He punches him in front of everyone, and then needles are found in his bag? Sounds like the fight might have been a cover for injecting him with poison."

"Those needles were for him," I protested. "He's got diabetes. And the fight was a long time before Cassar collapsed."

"Might have been slow-acting poison. I heard one of the doctors up at the hospital said it looked like cyanide.

Apparently Cassar was vomiting when he got to hospital and then he started having seizures."

"Goodness! How awful. But cyanide's not a very slow one, is it?" My knowledge of cyanide poisoning was limited to what I'd learned reading detective novels. "And how can they be sure the poison was injected? They'll need to do an autopsy. It might have been in his food or drink." That seemed more likely to me, considering the timing of his collapse and the fact that he lived long enough to reach the hospital.

"Maybe, but it doesn't look good, does it?" Denise's eyes gleamed. "On one side you've got a guy with a grudge who picks a fight at a wedding and carries needles, and on the other you've got a guy who dies of cyanide poisoning. Mighty suspicious, if you ask me."

CHAPTER 7

On the way home, I dropped into Heidi's shop, Toy Stories, to say hello. Rufus very begrudgingly sat on command outside the door. When I told him to stay, he gave me a look that said he was the saddest, most put-upon dog in the whole of Australia. I laughed and went inside.

Toy Stories was the kind of place guaranteed to lift your spirits—full of brightly coloured toys, its walls lined with children's books. In pride of place on the wall behind the counter was a canvas of one of my photos, featuring Heidi's twin boys leaping for joy with the blue sky behind them. I'd done a beach shoot with Heidi and her family recently, and that image captured the spirit of childhood so perfectly that that one photo was bringing me plenty of business.

That photo was a constant, but Heidi changed the decorations every month to keep the shop looking fresh and inviting. This month she'd chosen a fairy theme and there were tinsel garlands hanging from the roof with fairy dolls dangling from them. Pink fairy tutus and glittering silver wands were strung up everywhere and Heidi herself was wearing a fairy crown over her blond hair, which was in its customary plaited pigtails. She was the only grown woman I'd ever known who could get away with pigtails. On her it looked delightful—it suited her bubbly personality.

"Charlie! I haven't seen you in ages," she cried as I came in, the bell on the door announcing my presence. Heidi was a member of the book club Aunt Evie had dragged me to as soon as I moved in, and one of the nicest people I'd ever met. Possibly one of the nicest people ever, full stop. "I was only saying to Dave last night that I really needed to check up on you and see how you were going. How's the neck?"

"Much better, thanks. I haven't worn the brace in over a week. I think I'm pretty much back to normal."

She eyed me suspiciously. "What about the headaches?"

"Still getting a few, but they're not as bad as before."

"Well, that's good news. Just don't overdo it. I saw Priya yesterday. She was saying we should get together for drinks. It's too long until the next book club meeting."

Priya worked for the local newspaper, the *Sunny Bay Star*. Not surprisingly for someone whose job involved interviewing a lot of people, she was very social.

"Well, now that the wedding's over, I have nothing else on my calendar."

Heidi sighed. "I heard what happened. What an awful thing. And it sounds like it was a beautiful wedding up until that."

"It was. They were very lucky with the weather."

"Priya showed me some photos. Everyone looked so lovely."

"You wouldn't believe how long it took to get everyone looking that good. Molly is ..." A monster? A bridezilla? I tried to think of a nice way of putting it. "A bit of a perfectionist. The hair stylist had to do her hair three times before she was satisfied." I didn't mention the shouting and the tears, and how long she'd kept everyone waiting on the sand in the hot sun for her to arrive.

"That's because she has such good taste," Heidi said. Clearly my friend had never met the real Molly. "Did you know she designed her own engagement ring? She got Randall Clifford in Waterloo Bay to make it for her."

I whistled. I'd seen the shop and I doubted I could afford even to set foot inside it. "Ooh, exclusive."

"I think he was a little miffed that she wanted him to make her design. Usually he designs things himself. But she was willing to pay to get what she wanted."

"Well, every bride wants everything to be perfect for her big day," I said diplomatically.

"So how did the photos turn out?"

"Really well! I was so pleased."

"Any chance we can have a look?"

"I've sent the link to the online gallery to Molly. I figure she should probably see them first. But I'm sure she'll share it with everyone. Do you know when she'll be back from the honeymoon?"

"We can ask Sarah. Sarah!" she called into the depths of the shop. "Look who's here! It's Charlie."

Moments later Sarah appeared, her arms full of board books. She looked a lot less glamorous than when I'd last seen her in her bridesmaid's dress, but also a lot more stressed, with big dark circles under her eyes.

"Hi, Charlie." She smiled, but it looked like an effort.

"How are you?" I asked, immediately concerned.

"I've been better." She shrugged, then turned to Heidi, depositing the books on the counter. "Which ones do you think I should get? I can't decide."

"Who is it for?" I asked.

"One of the girls at work is having a baby shower. Everyone else will be getting her nappies and bottles and practical things. I thought I'd get a couple of books instead."

"Spoken like a true book club member," I said. "Andrea would be so proud."

Heidi laughed and helped her choose two from the pile that she said would be more suitable for a young baby because of their bright colours.

"When are Molly and Marco back?" she asked as she rang up the purchase.

"Thursday, I think. Marco couldn't get long off work, so it's a short honeymoon."

"That's a shame," Heidi said, "but I guess he only just started in that job, didn't he?"

"Yes," Sarah said, her face darkening. "The company hasn't been around long. And now his boss is dead, who knows if he even has a job to come back to?"

"Such a terrible thing," Heidi said, nodding.

"Terrible?" Sarah laughed, a short, bitter sound. "Couldn't have happened to a more deserving person. I'd be cheering if Troy wasn't the police's prime suspect."

"Why did Troy attack him on the beach like that?" I asked.

"Because the guy shoved him, like the jerk that he is. Was. We both hated him. Ben Cassar was a liar and a thief, and he's the reason that Troy and I are still living in my mother's spare bedroom."

Heidi leaned on the counter, a sympathetic look on her face. I guessed she knew what this was about, but it was all news to me. Before the wedding, I'd never spoken to Sarah about anything except whatever book we were discussing in our book club.

"Why?" I asked. "What happened?"

"What happened? He took our money for the house he was supposed to be building for us and spent it on overseas trips and fancy cars instead, that's what happened."

"And probably on that nasty little piece he was sleeping with, too," Heidi added.

"Yes. And we weren't the only ones he did it to. For months he promised that the bricks were on their way, or the scaffolding, or whatever the next thing was we were waiting for, while the build time dragged on and on and on and we still had no house. And then the company went broke and shut down, and we were left with half a house and no money to pay anyone else to finish it."

"That's awful!" I frowned. "But if the company went broke, how is he back in business again? Aren't there rules against that sort of thing?"

"He declared himself bankrupt—but all the assets were in his wife's name, so they've still got money. But we couldn't get anything unless we signed some stupid Deed of Company Arrangement—and then it turned out there was barely anything to split between all the people he owed money to anyway."

"But I thought you couldn't be a director again if you'd gone bankrupt or something."

"I guess he's not a director this time, just an employee. Look up the bankruptcy rules. It's an absolute disgrace, but perfectly legal, apparently."

"Who do you think could have murdered him?" Heidi asked.

Sarah shrugged. "Could have been anyone. We aren't the only ones he left high and dry, but he gets off scot-free. People see him still driving around town in his expensive car, living in that big house, and they hate him."

"So you think someone killed him for revenge?" I asked. "Doesn't that seem a little extreme?"

Heidi shook her head in wonder. "It makes me feel like I'm living in a thriller novel."

"I know, right? Surely in real life people don't do things like that?"

"I don't know," Heidi said. "I could imagine killing

someone for revenge if they murdered my kids or something, but not over money."

"Well, *I* wouldn't do it," Sarah said, "and Troy certainly didn't do it, either. But it wouldn't surprise me if someone did."

Heidi still looked doubtful. "According to statistics, in most murder cases, the killer is someone close to the victim. Usually someone with something to gain."

"Could be his wife, then," Sarah said. "I never did like Gail. She was a couple of years ahead of me at high school and she was a stuck-up cow even then."

"Being a cow doesn't make her a killer, though," I said. "Wouldn't divorce be easier?"

Sarah snorted as she gathered up her parcel. "Ask Andrea how easy divorce is. I reckon getting rid of a jerk of a husband without having to split all the assets would be a big bonus. I don't care who killed him; I'm just worried the police will try to pin it on Troy. Can you help us, Charlie? You solved Peggy's murder when the police were looking in the completely wrong direction. I'm sure you'd be able to figure it out, and I'm starting to feel like we need someone on our side."

"But surely they're not seriously looking at Troy?" I asked. "I know there was a bit of push and shove on the beach, but they can't really think he injected Cassar with poison. Those needles were for insulin."

"Well, of course."

"And there was probably too much time between the fight and the time of death for that to make sense anyway."

"Do they think he injected him later on?" Heidi asked doubtfully.

"Who knows what they think? But there's just one other little problem."

"What's that?"

"Troy threatened to kill him once before."

CHAPTER 8

AUNT EVIE AND I MET FOR LUNCH AT THE SURF CLUB CAFÉ. RUFUS stayed home this time, since he was stretched out in the sun in my little courtyard, fast asleep, when I left. He looked so cute I didn't have the heart to wake him.

I arrived before her, for a change, and took a seat outside under one of the big white umbrellas at a small table for two. We hadn't eaten here in a while—since before my car accident, in fact.

My hand crept to my neck as memories of the crash came back to me. Fortunately, I'd come through it with nothing more than a concussion and a bit of whiplash, but it had been a terrifying experience. So much so that I hadn't been behind the wheel of a car since.

Aunt Evie strode down the sandy path from the car park, dressed in a fifties-style pea-green dress with white polkadots. I stood up to give her a hug and a kiss. She only came up to my shoulder, tiny as a ballerina and always glamorous. Large crystal earrings dangled from her earlobes like chandeliers. People often mistook us for mother and daughter, as we had the same blue eyes and light-brown hair, though her hair colour owed more to a bottle than to nature these days.

"You look like Audrey Hepburn today," I told her. "Very stylish."

"Thank you, darling." She rubbed at the lipstick print her kiss had left on my cheek, then settled herself in the chair opposite me. The café was set up on the side of the surf club building and I'd left her the chair that faced the ocean.

She eyed me critically. "You're not wearing your neck brace today?"

"I haven't worn it for the last week."

"Is that wise?"

"The doctor said I only had to wear it as long as I felt I needed it, and my neck is feeling so much better. It's almost back to normal."

"Hmm." She picked up her menu but didn't look at it, instead continuing to study me over the top of it. "And how are you feeling otherwise? I heard Molly's wedding was a touch more exciting than it should have been. Did you see what happened?"

I picked up my own menu and shrugged. "There wasn't really anything to see. Apparently the toxicology report has come back saying it was cyanide, but I didn't notice anyone pouring poison into his drink, if that's what you mean."

She gave me an impatient look. "I mean, did he drop

dead on the spot? That must have been very upsetting for everyone."

I shook my head. "No, everyone thought he'd had a heart attack at first. He collapsed, but then he was able to walk from the room with a bit of help from the waiters. The ambulance came and took him to hospital. I guess they figured out when he got there and started seizing that it wasn't his heart after all."

"What a way to go. I didn't have much time for Ben Cassar but nobody would wish that kind of thing on their worst enemy."

I cocked an eyebrow at her. "Well, somebody must have. He didn't poison himself."

"That's true."

A waitress came to take our order. I asked for the Thai beef salad and Aunt Evie chose grilled vegetables on toasted sourdough. I thought we might move on to other topics after that, but Aunt Evie picked right back up where we'd left off as soon as the waitress went inside.

"I heard the police went straight into interviewing the chefs and servers. Ridiculous! As if Peter Bunning would be destroying his own livelihood by poisoning the meals he cooked. What possible motive could he have for attacking one of the guests?"

"In all fairness, he might have a motive, we just don't know what it is. But I would have thought the logistics of the situation would rule the chefs out. How would they know who would get which meal? It wasn't as if they were colour-coded or anything. They were all the same and the waiters just picked them up at random, as far as I could see."

"Oh, you were in the kitchen?"

I nodded. "I had my dinner in there. The head chef—Peter Bunning?—went off at one of the under-chefs about the chicken not being cooked through properly. A man who was so worried about the guests getting food poisoning doesn't seem to me like the type to outright murder someone."

"I've known Peter for years. He doesn't seem like the killing type to me, either."

"Plus, he'd have to be in league with one of the waiters, to make sure that the poisoned meal got to the right person, and that seems a very risky way of doing things. They could easily mess up and give the meal to the wrong person unless the poison one looked very different, which it probably couldn't or people would notice. And that's assuming the poison was even in the meal. It could have been in his drink, for all we know."

"In which case, it seems far more likely that the murderer would have been one of the waiters," Aunt Evie said. "Unless you think it's true that Troy Chapman stabbed him with a needle during a fight?"

The waitress returned with our drinks—a cappuccino for Aunt Evie and a pot of green tea for me. I took a sip and immediately wondered if I should have got a cold drink instead. It wasn't set to be a scorcher today but it was pretty warm here in the sun, even with the shade of the umbrella. December and the searing hot Australian summer was just around the corner.

"It was honestly just one punch. I can't see how he could have stabbed him with anything. There was a whole bunch of people watching. And Ben didn't collapse until a couple of hours later, which seems too long. Much more likely it was something in the food or drink. But, speaking of waiters ... There was a waitress there, a blond girl, who swapped tables with one of the other waiters so she wouldn't have to serve Ben and his wife. Emma or Ella. She said she'd just been fired by them. She broke down when she heard that Ben was dead."

"Oh, that would be Ella Giordano," Aunt Evie said, sipping her coffee. "The gossip was all over town a couple of weeks ago. She was Ben's receptionist. Apparently, she and Ben had been having an affair all year. Gail found out about it and insisted she be sacked." Her eyes lit up. "She could be after revenge."

"Wouldn't she'd kill *Gail* if she was after revenge? And why would she swap tables if she wanted to poison one of them? That just makes it harder. But she seemed so upset at his death I can't believe she killed him. It looked to me like she still loved him. And I saw Ben watching her at one point in the evening, so I reckon he was still interested, too."

"Very likely, but then Ben's been interested in plenty of women other than the one he was married to over the years. He wasn't known for his fidelity. Perhaps he was using Gail's discovery as an excuse to get out of an affair he was no longer interested in. You know what they say about spurned women," she said darkly.

I laughed. "Aunt Evie, you sound like something out of

a TV melodrama. How is she supposed to have poisoned him from the other side of the room?"

"I'm sure I don't know. Perhaps she had an accomplice, and swapping tables was meant as a kind of alibi. Or perhaps she and Ben had a secret tryst in the bathroom between courses and she did the deed then."

"Are you so determined to make her guilty? I almost feel sorry for her. I mean, obviously she shouldn't have been having an affair with a married man, but she just lost her job and now she's lost the man she loves, too. That's pretty tough."

Aunt Evie leaned back in her chair, eyebrows raised. "I'm surprised to hear you, of all people, excuse someone for an affair."

"I'm not excusing her. I'm just saying she's had a tough time."

"So are you going to investigate?"

"What?" I set my teacup down and it rattled in the saucer. "Why is everyone asking me that? I'm not a detective."

"Why, who else asked you?"

"Sarah. I saw her earlier in Toy Stories. She's worried about Troy's involvement."

"Bah." Aunt Evie waved her hand airily, dismissing him as a suspect. "He was always a hot-head, even as a child. Sweet boy, though. I can't see him poisoning anyone, even a repulsive creature like Ben Cassar."

"Unfortunately, he's made things tougher for himself by threatening to kill Cassar."

"At the wedding?"

"No, last year. Very publicly, too. Apparently, at the first creditors' meeting after Ben's business went bust, Troy had to be restrained from assaulting Ben."

Aunt Evie sighed. "It seems to be a pattern for him."

"Yes. And while they were dragging him away, he was shouting some rather graphic death threats. The police were called and Troy spent several hours at the station cooling off, though Cassar made a big man of himself and declined to press charges. So if you add that history to motive, Troy starts to look very suspicious." I poured the last of my green tea into my cup, thinking of Sarah's worried face. "Although where they think Troy would get his hands on cyanide, I don't know."

"Well, he does work at a lab."

"He does?" I stopped contemplating my tea and met Aunt Evie's eyes, shocked. "Sarah didn't tell me that." Was she being protective, or trying to hide something? "What lab? Do they keep cyanide there?"

Aunt Evie shrugged. "I have no idea. You should ask Sarah."

"I will." I shook my head. "That does look bad for Troy. No wonder she wants help—though surely a lawyer would be more use than I would."

"Don't sell yourself short, dear. You did such a good job finding Peggy's killer."

Peggy had been Aunt Evie's friend and next-door neighbour. Somehow Aunt Evie had managed to twist my arm into looking into what she insisted was a murder when everyone else said her friend had died of natural causes. As usual, it turned out that Aunt Evie's intuition was correct.

"That's what Sarah said."

"I still don't believe Troy did it. He may be impulsive, but he's not *stupid*. Why would he pick a fight with the man at the wedding and make himself the prime suspect if he was already planning to murder him by stealth a couple of hours later?" Aunt Evie took a sip of coffee, then set her cup down with a decisive air. "I bet it was the wife. We should break in and search her house for cyanide."

I choked on a mouthful of tea and put the cup down, coughing desperately to clear my airways. "Aunt Evie! We are not breaking into anyone's house. That's illegal!"

"So?" She flashed me a mischievous grin. "No one's going to arrest a sweet little old lady."

"I'll give you the *little*. But as for sweet—or old! The word you're looking for is *crazy*." I pointed my fork at her with the sternest expression I could muster. "Don't you dare do anything of the sort."

"Although I don't know why she'd choose to do the deed at the wedding," she mused, completely ignoring me. "Much riskier, with all those witnesses, than doing it in the comfort of her own home."

"Probably so there'd be lots of other suspects. At home, she's the only one, isn't she? What's she going to say when the police come knocking? *Whoops, I must have mixed up the cyanide and the garlic again. Silly me!*"

She laughed. "True. Well, perhaps it *was* Troy. Men can be so deceptive." She put her knife and fork down and gave me that piercing Aunt Evie look, the one that said she wouldn't let a topic go until she had answers she found satisfactory. I quailed a little inside. "And speaking of deceptive men, let's change the subject. What on earth is going on with Will and these flowers? Don't send any more to Sunrise Lodge, for goodness sake. We have flowers coming out our ears. I've given them to everyone I can think of."

I sighed, glancing down at my Thai beef salad. It really was delicious, with mingled flavours of ginger, peanut, and coriander, but this turn of conversation was making me lose my appetite. "I wish he'd stop. It's driving me crazy, too."

"You'll just have to talk to him," Aunt Evie declared with typical resolution. "There's no sense letting it drag on if it's making you miserable. You know what a stubborn man he can be."

"I know." I shut my eyes, letting the warmth of the sun soak into me. "I just don't want to have to deal with him right now, on top of everything else."

"Everything else?" She gave me a shrewd look. "You mean the accident?"

"Not just that. Starting up a new business, feeling sore all the time. Having to carry my groceries home on foot."

"Surely your insurance company should have supplied a rental car until your new car is ready? I thought you had a full replacement policy?"

"They offered, but I turned it down."

"Turned it down?" There was a short pause, then she said in a softer tone, "You're scared to drive again, aren't you?"

She looked unexpectedly like Mum with that understanding expression on her face. Mum had been a much softer person than her big sister. The sudden reminder hit me with a fierce stab of longing. What wouldn't I give for one more of her hugs?

I cleared my throat, blinking away a sudden dampness as I stared at the table. "I'm sure I'll be fine by the time the new car is delivered. I just thought a little break wouldn't do me any harm."

"Charlotte Rose Carter, my sister didn't raise any spineless children. It's like riding a horse—you should have got straight back behind the wheel. Now you've built it up into something frightening. Like this reluctance to talk to Will. You know what has to be done, just get in there and do it. You'll be glad when it's not hanging over your head anymore."

"Yes, Aunt Evie." What else could I say?

CHAPTER 9

I SAT IN THE SUN IN MY LITTLE COURTYARD NEXT MORNING, eating peanut butter on toast. Our book club was reading another Jane Austen novel, *Sense and Sensibility*, for our next book. I'd borrowed it from Heidi, and it lay open on the table next to my plate, but I was having trouble focusing on reading. I hadn't slept too well the night before and the sunshine was making me sleepy.

I'd had the nightmare again, the one where I crashed the car into the cliff face, just as I had in real life, only this time no Curtis turned up to help me out of the car to safety. In the dream, it was the killer who opened my door, knife in hand, and dragged me screaming from the wreckage. I always woke up at that point, but that was quite scary enough to keep me awake for several hours. Last night I'd even got up and walked around the house checking all the locks on the windows and doors, though I knew perfectly well that the killer was in jail awaiting trial and couldn't possibly harm me.

As a result, the trials and tribulations of Elinor and Marianne weren't enough to hold my interest this morning, though I'd been enjoying the book last night before I went to sleep. I felt sorry for Elinor—she was so sensible and pragmatic that it must have been hard for her to deal with the flighty Marianne, even though it was clear she loved her sister very much. I'd always wanted a sister, but only had Adam, and it had been over a year since I'd seen him, anyway. He was on the other side of the world in California, making money hand over fist in some tech company, and didn't have much time for chatting to his sister, though he would eventually answer my emails if I was persistent enough.

A black nose appeared under the fence that separated my little courtyard from Mrs Johnson's next door. It was quickly followed by chocolate brown eyes and then a whole furry head.

"Good morning!" I said.

There was a hole there that didn't seem anywhere near big enough for a fully grown golden retriever, but Rufus wriggled and squirmed his way through on a regular basis.

With one last heave, he popped out of the hole and shook himself, then trotted over to me, wagging his tail. With perfect manners, he sat down at my feet and looked meaningfully at the toast in my hand. I paused, the piece of toast halfway to my lips, and laughed.

"Oh, I see. This isn't just a social call. You're actually after food. Why am I not surprised?" Could he have smelled the peanut butter all the way from the other side of the fence? Probably, since a dog's sense of smell was so much better than a human's. I took another bite and Rufus watched me, unblinking, absolutely convinced that the delights of peanut butter toast were wasted on me.

"Would you like some of this?" I waved the toast slowly from side to side and watched him track it with utmost concentration. "You would, wouldn't you? Are you a good boy? Do you *deserve* a piece of toast?"

His tail thumped against the pavers at the sound of my voice, which I supposed was answer enough. He was the most deserving good boy ever, and would cherish that toast in a way that I, a mere human, couldn't possibly. When there was only a small square of toast left, I tossed it to him and he snatched it out of the air with glee.

I thought he would swallow it whole, but much chewing ensued. After a moment, I realised that he'd caught it peanut butter side up, and now the small piece of toast was wedged against the roof of his mouth. He chomped and chomped. And chomped some more. He didn't seem at all unhappy with the arrangement and I laughed again as he lay down in the sun, still chewing happily. Finally he managed to dislodge it and the chomping stopped, only to be replaced by enthusiastic licking of his chops. When he'd finished, he gazed at me hopefully, but I shook my head.

"There's no more, gorgeous." I held up my open hands, palms towards him, to show that they were empty. "All gone."

His ears drooped a little, then he rolled onto his back

and wriggled around, scratching his back against the pavers. I shook my head again, still smiling. Crazy dog.

The doorbell rang inside the house and he scrambled to his feet, instantly alert. I checked my watch and sighed.

"Don't fuss, boy. I know who this will be." Nevertheless, he trotted at my side through the house to the front door.

It was Steve, of course, with another big bunch of roses. Their soft pink reminded me of the flowers from Molly's wedding. I had spent a lot of time over the past few days looking at photos with those flowers.

"Morning," Steve said, offering them to me. "How are you today? I see you've got a new friend. I didn't know you had a dog."

"Oh, he's not mine. He lives next door, but he likes to visit."

Steve laughed. "I *thought* he looked a lot like Rufus. Well, have a good day. I guess I'll be seeing you again tomorrow."

I closed the door behind him and Rufus and I headed back out to the courtyard, where the last of my morning coffee awaited me. I wondered if Rufus was thirsty, after that epic bout with the peanut butter. I stopped in the kitchen, dumping the flowers on the bench, and digging out an old plastic bowl that I could fill with water for him.

"There you go," I said as I set the bowl down on the pavers outside the back door. Rufus took a long and very noisy drink, which suggested that he had indeed been thirsty. I sat back down and picked up *Sense and Sensibility* but after rereading the same paragraph three or four times

I had to admit that I wasn't really in the mood for Mari-anne's fictional romantic troubles at the moment. I could see the roses on my bench from here, a sad reminder that I had enough romantic troubles of my own.

I really had to ring Will and put a stop to this once and for all. I had nothing against Steve, but I didn't want to meet him on my doorstep every morning like this for weeks. This had gone on long enough. I could be an Elinor, practical and clear-eyed in facing unpleasant necessities.

I picked up the phone and found Will's number in my contacts, even though I had it memorised. And then I stopped, just staring at his name on the screen. For a long moment, I sat frozen, until Rufus wandered over and dripped cold water on my bare foot. I patted his silken head absentmindedly.

"Don't be such a sook," I told myself. "You can do this. Come on, Rufus, let's go for a walk."

Rufus's ears pricked at the word *walk* and he stood up, his silky tail wagging, his claws clicking on the pavers as he turned tight, excited circles. I put on my shoes and grabbed my camera bag and we set off.

What was I afraid of? Not Will, of course. I was the injured party, as the flowers attested. And if he started trying to persuade me to get back together with him again, I could just hang up. It wasn't like the time he'd shown up here unannounced. I'd felt trapped then, even though we were outside on the driveway. He was a forceful personality, and it was hard to say no to him in person once he had set his mind on something. I wavered long enough that the phone screen went dark and then, impatient at my own cowardice, I stabbed at the screen and called his number before I could change my mind.

He answered almost immediately, putting paid to my hopes that I could just leave a message telling him where to stick his flowers.

"Charlie!" His familiar voice made a hollow open in my stomach. "It's so good to hear from you."

I couldn't reply straight away. That voice. The way it lifted with a happy energy as he said my name. Until a few short weeks ago, this man had been my world. My future.

And then he slept with your best friend, I reminded myself sternly as we turned the corner onto Beach Road. *There's no going back after that.*

Will had destroyed that future. No one had held a gun at his head and forced him to sleep with Amy. He'd made a deliberate choice. He couldn't act now as if that was some little slip that could be explained away. He hadn't forgotten my birthday or left the toilet seat up. He'd betrayed me, lied about it, and destroyed my trust.

"Please stop sending me flowers," I said, and immediately hated myself for that *please*. He didn't deserve politeness.

"But I don't want to stop. You deserve flowers. You deserve anything you want."

"What I *deserve* is for you to stop sending me flowers and just leave me alone."

"I can't do that," he said promptly. "I love you, Charlie. Just let me prove it to you."

"I don't want to discuss this."

Rufus looked up at me with a happy doggy smile and I

stroked his flippy-floppy ears absent-mindedly, grateful for his comforting presence at my side. My heart was racing from the unpleasant emotions this conversation was stirring up.

"We need to talk," Will said. "I'll come to your house."

"No, don't!" I said in knee-jerk horror. I couldn't stand having him invading my space. "We don't need to talk. I have nothing to say to you."

"But I have plenty to say to you, and I'll keep sending flowers until you hear me out."

That was classic Will. He didn't like taking no for an answer. Unfortunately, I knew he was telling the truth—those damn flowers would keep arriving if I didn't give him what he wanted.

"Aren't you in Sydney, at work?" I walked faster, as if I could somehow escape Will that way. "We can do this on the phone, if you insist."

"Actually I'm in Sunrise Bay at the moment. Just got in last night. Where shall we meet? How about dinner at the Metropole tonight? That's where I'm staying."

Of course he was. The Metropole was a little past its best, but it was still a beautiful—and expensive—place to stay, the grandest accommodation in tiny Sunrise Bay. Naturally, Will would be staying there rather than some beachside motel or Airbnb where he'd have to look after himself. Nothing but the best for Will Harris. He probably had a suite.

"No." Dinner was too much of a commitment. "I'll meet you at the surf club café for a coffee on Thursday. Ten o'clock."

"Thursday? What about tomorrow?"

"I'm busy." I wasn't, but I wasn't going to jump just because Will snapped his fingers. He could wait an extra day.

I hung up without saying goodbye, which gave me a certain childish satisfaction. Rufus circled back to me from sniffing at a telegraph pole, and gazed up at me with those soulful brown eyes. I needed a man who looked at me with that kind of adoration. Dogs really were better than people.

Striding out briskly, we headed through the little town and up the hill towards Sunrise Lodge. But today we weren't going to see Aunt Evie; my goal was in the streets beyond the retirement village.

Right up on the headland, in the ritziest street in Sunny Bay, was a row of luxury houses. Several of them were owned by wealthy people from Sydney and used as holiday homes, but there were a few that had permanent residents. The view of the bay from up here was spectacular, and the house I stopped at was a modern, boxy dwelling with vast sheets of glass facing the ocean. Architect-designed, for sure, with four garages for all the fancy cars.

After a minute to catch my breath from the climb, I knocked on the door. Rufus was happily poking around in some bushes on the other side of the street. I hoisted the strap of my camera bag to a more comfortable position and listened to the sound of high heels tapping on tiles approach.

Gail Cassar opened her door and stared at me with no

recognition. Behind her I caught a glimpse of an enormous, white-tiled foyer with a large fishpond set into the floor. "Yes?"

"Hi, I'm Charlie Carter, the photographer from the wedding." I unzipped the pocket of my bag and pulled out a photo. "I brought you this. I thought you might like to have it. I'm very sorry for your loss."

It was the photo of table ten. I'd picked the best one of Gail there was; she looked slightly less disdainful in this shot. Nick's friend Larry had his eyes shut, but I doubted Gail would care about that.

She gazed at the last photo ever taken of her husband, then looked up at me expressionlessly. Her makeup was flawless, her eyes clear. She certainly didn't look like a woman mired in grief. "Thanks."

"How are you coping?" I asked.

Her eyes narrowed. "You're new around here, aren't you?"

What an odd thing to say. "Yes?"

"You must be the only person in town who doesn't think I'm celebrating."

"I'm sure no one—"

She cut me off. "I know what they're all whispering. They think I killed him. I bet they're all feeling sorry for poor little Ella right now. How sad! How heartbroken! She's a good actress, I'll give her that. But they'll find out the truth soon enough."

"The truth? What's that?"

"That Ella Giordano doesn't take no for an answer. She killed my husband."

CHAPTER 10

Gail shut the door on me without another word, leaving me bemused on her luxurious doorstep.

"Come on, Rufus, let's go."

She thought Ella had killed Ben? I would have loved to ask why, but having the door slammed in my face was a pretty fair indication that Gail wasn't in a chatty mood. I'd been hoping to get a little more out of her, but I'd just have to figure it out for myself.

Rufus and I stopped at the end of the street to take photos looking south across the bay. I could see the roof of my house from here, so far away it was a miniature dolls' house on the far shore. A pair of windsurfers played in the waves off the southern headland, their colourful sails tiny against the vastness of the blue water, even with my tele-photo lens.

"Do you fancy a walk to the other side?" I asked the dog. I'd love to get some closer shots of the bright orange and yellow sails.

He trotted off ahead of me, which I took as agreement.

We had passed Sunrise Lodge and were almost down on the flat again when a flock of cockatoos flew screeching overhead and landed in the grass at the end of the street. They looked like giant flowers with their big white bodies and cheerful yellow crests, bobbing about in the grass looking for seeds. Rufus watched them with interest, ears pricked and tail straight out behind him. As he got closer, he began to move more deliberately, placing each paw carefully, never taking his eyes from the birds. They, of course, took absolutely no notice of him.

I laughed. "You're kidding yourself, dog."

There was no way he could catch one. They might look as though they were ignoring him—they were quite bold and barely hopped out of the way when people passed by —but they could hardly fail to notice twenty-five kilos of fluffy stupidity prowling towards them. Rufus might have the hunt in his blood but he wasn't exactly *subtle*. No self-respecting cockatoo would stand around waiting to become a Rufus snack.

He was barely four feet away when they finally decided enough was enough and took flight. He pounced, and to my absolute astonishment managed to trap one clumsily half under his chest. I didn't know who was more surprised—Rufus, the bird, or me.

He looked up at me in shock, as if to say, *What do I do now?*

I hurried forward. "Rufus, you idiot, get off it!"

He hadn't even attempted to bite it. For him, the game was all in the chase—he'd probably been doing this for years without ever catching one, and now he was flummoxed. I pushed him, and the bird, which had been lying quietly until now, squawked. He flinched away, and the cockatoo wasted no time in making its escape, taking to the sky so rapidly it was clear nothing had been damaged except its pride.

Nothing remained except a couple of yellow-tinged white feathers. He sniffed at them doubtfully, then trotted off down the street, tail held at a jaunty angle. *Look at me, the conquering hero!*

"Going to brag to all your friends about what a big, bad hunter you are, are you?"

He ignored me, and I followed the jaunty tail all the way through the town and up the hill to the top of the southern headland, which took a good half hour of brisk walking. I'd had more exercise in the last few weeks of living in Sunny Bay than I'd had all last year in Sydney. If I kept this up I'd have muscles to rival Curtis's.

Well, maybe not. That man was *built.*

A little farther on, the road took some tight curves around the cliff edge, where I'd had my car accident, but we weren't going that far today. Instead my goal was a green patch of bush that hugged the promontory, giving a glorious view of the ocean below from the shade of the tall gums. The council had obligingly built some wooden walkways so that people could admire the view without getting mud up to their ankles in wet weather. It should be a prime spot to photograph the windsurfers.

The track widened into a lookout at the most easterly point, giving a view up and down the coastline. Apparently if you came in the right season you could catch a glimpse of whales passing in their annual migration, but so far I hadn't seen anything more exciting than a group of surfers or a small boat.

Rufus lolloped ahead, his stride deceptively slow, but I couldn't keep up without breaking into a jog. And it was far too hot today for jogging. He disappeared around a bend and barked a couple of times. He'd probably found a goanna sunning itself on a tree, or even another cockatoo. Two in one day would make him immensely pleased with himself.

But when I rounded the bend I drew in a sharp breath. There was a metal fence around the lookout, about chest height, and he was facing it, the flag of his tail waving uncertainly. On the other side of the fence, facing the deadly drop to the rocks below, was a woman in workout gear, her bright blond hair tied back in a loose ponytail that fluttered in the salty sea breeze.

"Careful!" I cried, rushing to the fence. "You're too close to the edge."

There was a big warning sign right in front of me—she couldn't have failed to see it. *Danger: no access past this point. Cliff edge is unstable.*

She looked back and a shock of recognition ran through me. It was Ella Giordano, and she'd been crying. What was she *doing* out there? I hoisted myself up onto the top of the railing, filled with a sudden horrible certainty that she meant to throw herself from the cliff.

"Ella! Come back!" I landed awkwardly on the other side and stopped, fighting the temptation to lunge at her and grab hold. If I spooked her she might jump. Behind me Rufus whined.

She sniffed and scrubbed at her face. "I won't be a minute. Just have to grab my hat."

She inched carefully towards the long grasses that waved in the wind right on the edge of the cliff. A white baseball cap was caught on a bush there. So she hadn't been about to jump—the wind had just blown her hat off. The woman was nuts. That grass was practically the only thing holding the crumbling sandstone of the cliff edge together. It was only a hat, for goodness sake. You could buy a new one for less than five dollars in half a dozen places in Sunny Bay. Was it really worth risking life and limb to retrieve it?

"Give me your hand," I said, reaching out for her with one hand, the other closed in a death grip on the reassuring metal of the fence behind me. There was no way *I* was going over that edge for the sake of a stupid hat. The sea wind buffeted my face, filling my nostrils with salt and whipping my hair around my head. "Don't get so close to the edge. It's not safe."

"It's fine," she said, snatching the white hat with one hand before retreating back to the fence and safety. She wiped again at her tear-streaked face and eyed me sideways. "Don't I know you?"

I waited until she had boosted herself to the top of the fence before clambering over myself. Rufus nuzzled my hand in greeting and I patted his sun-warmed head, my hand shaking just a little. I was scared of heights, okay? "I was the photographer at Molly and Marco's wedding on

Saturday. I was there in the kitchen when the police told us about Ben."

Recognition appeared in her eyes. "Oh."

"I'm sorry for your loss."

She crossed her arms tightly over her generous chest, cap still clutched firmly in one hand, and laughed. It was not a happy sound. "You know, you're the first person who's been sorry for *my* loss? Everyone else is giving their sympathy to that monster he married. It's absolutely wasted on her. She's probably *glad* that he's dead."

Her defensive posture and the angry pain in her face softened my heart towards her. She may have been the "other woman", but she had clearly loved the guy.

"She certainly didn't seem very happy with him from what I saw at the wedding," I agreed cautiously. Gail *said* she wasn't celebrating. I'd take her word for it and assume she must have loved him at one point.

"She was never happy. Nothing he did was ever good enough for her, but she still refused to let him go."

"Why?" That kind of behaviour was so foreign to me. I'd walked out on Will the instant I'd realised he was in a relationship with another woman. Where was Gail's pride? "Most women wouldn't be happy living in that situation, knowing their husband would rather be with someone else."

Ella shrugged. "I guess she just liked the money too much. Everything was in her name because of the bankruptcy. If they'd got divorced she would have had to give him half. She liked making him suffer. And telling him what to do, like forcing him to break it off with me. She's a petty, vicious woman who likes having that kind of power over other people. You don't know what she's like—she is stone cold." The wind whipped at her blond hair, lashing strands of it into her face, and she raked them out of the way with impatient fingers. The salt air was cool in this exposed spot beyond the shelter of the trees. "Someone should have poisoned *her* instead."

"Oh, don't say that." I reached out, as if to push the words away. "Someone would take it the wrong way."

She gave another bitter laugh and jammed the cap onto her head, pulling her ponytail through the gap at the back with a vicious tug. "Oh, don't worry, that horrible detective is already convinced I poisoned Ben. I've told them everything I know, but he already dragged me in for two follow-up interviews and now he's talking about another one. I can tell he doesn't believe a word I say."

I was glad that Detective McGovern was at least looking at other suspects besides Troy. "I'm sure he's just following procedure."

"Huh. I don't know what possible reason he thinks I could have for murdering the love of my life. Ben was finally about to leave that witch he married—we had everything to look forward to. Trust me, if I'd been going to poison anyone at that stupid wedding, I would have picked Gail."

"It's hard to believe anyone could do something like that. Someone must have really hated him. Did he have any enemies?" Obviously, I knew the answer to that already, but I wanted to know what she'd say.

"Apart from Gail, you mean? I wouldn't put it past her. She probably decided she'd had enough."

I reached down and fondled Rufus's soft ears. He grinned happily up at me, his tongue lolling out one side of his mouth.

A jealous wife as the murderer had one big problem, considering what I'd heard about Ben's taste for affairs. Why now and not one of the many other times he'd cheated on her? Unless it was true that Ben had been about to leave her. I definitely had my doubts. Ben seemed like the type to promise everything and deliver nothing.

"Was there anyone else, though?" I pressed. "Anyone that might have had a reason to kill him? What about unhappy customers?" Sarah had told me that she and Troy weren't the only ones he'd stiffed with his Deed of Company Arrangement. Had he ripped off someone who was angry enough about it to kill?

She shrugged. "There were a few houses left unfinished when he restructured the company, but they should have had insurance."

Really? That seemed a callous attitude. And wasn't it the builder who was supposed to have the insurance?

"Were you working for him when he did the restructure?"

"Yes."

"What about suppliers and subcontractors? Did they all get paid?"

She shrugged. "They all got something. A couple of the subbies weren't happy, but that's business. It's no reason to kill someone. And most of them are back working for him again, so they can't be that upset. *Were* working for him," she corrected herself.

She looked like she might cry again, but I felt less sympathy now. She didn't seem to care that people had lost money because of her boyfriend's dodgy business practices.

"What about the ones that aren't back?" I persisted. "Are they still in business?"

Going bankrupt because your biggest customer refused to pay you for the work you'd done sounded like a pretty good motive for murder to me.

Ella gave me an odd look. "Why are you asking about this? Are you working with the police?" She took a step towards the path, as if she wasn't so keen to talk to me anymore.

"No. Just trying to put it all together in my head. Trying to understand how something like this can happen. Sunrise Bay seems like such a peaceful place—it's hard to believe people get murdered here. That's something you expect in a big city like Sydney."

She snorted. "People are still people, wherever they live. Sunrise Bay has just as many secrets as anywhere else."

Then she set off down the path, leaving me and Rufus alone with the salt-scented wind and the sound of the waves crashing against the rocks below.

CHAPTER 11

So that was two votes for Gail as the killer—Sarah and Ella. Two and a half, maybe, if you counted Aunt Evie, who would be happy to convict either Gail or Ella. In many ways, Gail made the most sense. If you asked who gained from Ben's death, Gail was the obvious answer. And she seemed like a pretty tough customer. She'd forced him to give up the woman he was having an affair with, she held all the purse strings, and she certainly seemed angry enough with him. I remembered how coolly she'd shrugged off his arm at the wedding, and how meekly he'd accepted it. Yes, she had definitely worn the pants in that relationship.

"Does that mean she was capable of murder?" I asked Rufus as we headed back along our street towards home. His ears pricked at the sound of my voice, but he was too engrossed in whatever he was sniffing to actually look at me.

It would take nerves of steel to sit next to the guy you were about to murder half the night, with a vial of cyanide tucked quietly into your purse. Did she slip it into his drink? She'd have to be so careful that no one saw her. It was hardly something you could explain away as something innocent.

What's this? Oh, just a little health tonic I like to add to Ben's drink. No, darling, of course it's not poison.

Maybe she'd done it when I'd been organising everyone for the photo. All the guests had been moving around, looking at me and not each other. If she'd been quick and confident, she could have tipped a couple of drops into his glass while everyone was distracted.

But it seemed such a risk—and I still wasn't sure that Gail was a likely suspect. Sure, she could rid herself of a cheating husband and ensure she kept all the money in one fell swoop, but I kept coming back to the question: why now? He'd been cheating on her for years, and she'd put up with it. Why would she suddenly decide to handle things differently?

According to what Ella had told me about her, it almost seemed as if she hadn't minded the affairs so much, because they gave her control over her husband. *She likes having control*, Ella had said. Was it because Ben had been about to leave her for Ella?

But I only had Ella's word for that. Even if that was something that she believed, I had serious doubts it was actually true. A man who'd had a dozen mistresses didn't suddenly decide to leave his wife for one of them. Especially not when that wife owned all his assets. Ben was the kind of guy who loved himself first and foremost, and it would be out of character for him to do something so thoroughly against his own best interests.

I unlocked my front door, and Rufus followed me in as if he belonged here. He was spending more and more time on this side of the fence lately. Maybe it had something to do with the yummy dog treats I'd bought for him.

I got one out and he immediately sat down, eager to prove he was a good boy and deserving of treats. He made short work of it while I made myself a coffee.

How had Ben felt about bowing to his wife's will, knowing that all his worldly assets were in her name? Was he scared she'd divorce him and he'd lose it all? Was that why he'd been bending over backwards to please her and get back in her good books?

Surely a man who was used to calling the shots at work wouldn't like being in that position in his private life. Maybe we had it all wrong, and *he'd* been trying to poison *her*, and he'd mixed up the drinks somehow.

"No, that's ridiculous." Rufus wagged, hoping another treat was forthcoming. "He'd have to be the most incompetent murderer in the world to drink his own poison, wouldn't he, boy?"

Yes, everyone had been moving around, but if you were going to add a deadly poison to someone's glass, there was no way you'd be casual enough to lose track of it in the confusion and end up drinking it yourself. It wasn't as if people swapped glasses willy nilly.

I wasn't even sure the poison had been in his drink. I wondered if Curtis would tell me if I asked him. Probably not. Detective McGovern wouldn't care to have details of his investigation spread around town.

There was more potential for confusion if the poison had been in the meal. I thought back to the moment—I'd been trying to organise the photo and the waiters had been swirling around the table: the tall guy Jimmy who'd swapped with Ella, the head waiter, and one other woman. They'd all had three or four plates balanced on their arms, and they'd been dodging passers-by as much as each other. Half the guests had been out of their places, chatting to people at other tables, or going to the bathroom or the bar, when dinner service had started.

Someone walking past could have added poison to one of the meals. Or one of the waiters could have done it. Half the people in the room could have had an opportunity.

"Okay, that's an exaggeration," I said to Rufus. He wagged, following me out to the courtyard, prepared to humour my habit of talking to myself. I sat down and stretched my legs out in front of me, savouring that first sip of coffee. "Maybe not half the room. But plenty of people could have had the chance."

It still seemed so risky, though. Who knew which of those meals would end up where, as the waiters danced around the table, dropping them in alternating order? Safer to wait until they'd actually been delivered, so you could be sure you were poisoning the right one.

But that was much harder to do discreetly, which put me right back where I started, with the difficulty of poisoning Ben's food without anyone catching the killer in the act. Really the only people who could have managed it were the ones sitting on either side of him—which again put Gail right at the top of the list of suspects.

"Surely it couldn't have been that cute old guy," I said to Rufus, who was stretched out on the warm pavers in the sun. He wagged lazily but didn't even open his eyes, much less raise his head to look at me.

Ben's neighbour at the table, with his neat red bowtie and cheeky grin, had seemed such a sweet old man. Surely he couldn't have had a reason to hate Ben?

I didn't even know his name. I pulled out my phone and rang Sarah. Had the police been to see him yet? I hoped the grumpy Detective McGovern hadn't been as short with him as he had with me. The poor old thing would be scared, wondering how he'd ended up a suspect in a murder case at his age, and not knowing what to do about it. Suddenly I really wanted to prove that he had had nothing to do with the murder.

"Sarah speaking."

"Hi, Sarah, it's Charlie. Can I ask you something about Molly's wedding?"

"Anything. Does that mean you're taking the case?"

I squirmed in my seat. She made me sound like some private eye in a trench coat. "Let's just say I'm looking at some possibilities. Do you know who that old guy was who was sitting next to Ben Cassar? He was tiny, all bent over and frail-looking. He had white hair and he was wearing a red bowtie."

"Oh, that would be Neville Botham. But Neville's not

the killer. He wouldn't hurt a fly."

"I'm sure you're right, but I'd still like to talk to him. I thought I might drop around a photo from the wedding for him. I got a lovely shot of him with Molly after dinner." That had worked to get Gail to talk to me, though not as well as I'd hoped. But it was still a good excuse to chat to people.

"That's a nice idea. I'm sure he'd appreciate it."

"How do you guys know him, anyway?"

"He used to live next door to us when we were growing up. He and his wife Joyce were lovely neighbours. We were always in there, begging scones from Joyce after school. She was the best cook."

"She's not around anymore?"

"No, sadly. She died when I was still in high school. Neville's been on his own for a while now. He moved into Sunrise Lodge a couple of years ago—he had a big garden and it got too much for him to manage. He's such a sweetheart. Their daughter was older than us. He and Joyce used to treat us like grandchildren. Man, I haven't thought of her scones in years. They were the best."

"And now I feel like scones. Thanks for that!"

She sighed. "I'll buy you all the scones you can eat if you can manage to find out who did this."

"Have the police spoken to Troy again?"

"No, but they told him not to leave town. Charlie, I'm so worried. I haven't been able to focus on work at all. I don't know how Troy keeps going."

"Maybe work distracts him from it. What does he do?"

"He works for the university down in Newcastle."

"As a lecturer?"

"As a researcher. Medical research."

"Ah. So he works in a lab?" Aunt Evie had said so, but it was good to get it straight from the horse's mouth.

"Yes."

"Do you know if they keep cyanide at the lab?"

"Detective McGovern asked about that, too. They only have a tiny amount, and it's kept locked up. Troy doesn't have access to it."

"Right." Troy *didn't* have access, or Troy wasn't *supposed* to have access? I bet Detective McGovern didn't believe that Troy was incapable of getting cyanide if he really wanted to. Poor Sarah. The case against Troy just kept getting stronger. "While I've got you, can I ask you some more about that Deed of Company Arrangement you were talking about?"

"What about it?"

"Do you know who else signed it? Seems like someone who was unhappy with the deal they got might have decided to bump Ben off."

She sighed. "I don't know who signed it, but I can tell you who was at the initial meeting of creditors. I think I still have the minutes somewhere in my files. Give me a second to fire up my laptop and I'll email it to you."

"Thanks."

I got out my own laptop in readiness, and a few minutes later a new email dropped into my inbox, with the minutes attached. I opened it up and scanned the list of attendees. None of the names were familiar to me, except for Sarah and Troy Chapman, and one other. And he was owed over $67,000 in unpaid subcontracting invoices. Ouch.

Nick Kettlewell.

CHAPTER 12

Nick and Ben Cassar had some history, Andrea had told me at the wedding. Sixty-seven thousand dollars' worth of history, apparently. That was quite a lot—but was it enough to kill someone for?

I sat on a low stone wall in Fenton Street, the main shopping street of Waterloo Bay, the next day. The sun beat down on my bare shoulders and radiated up off the pavement into my face. Across the road was Beach Bods, Waterloo Bay's biggest and most popular gym. I watched its smoky glass doors and thought back to what else Andrea had told me about Nick Kettlewell. Not much, really. I'd been too busy teasing her about Mr Darcy.

She'd met him at Beach Bods, where they sometimes had coffee together after a workout. He was a carpenter and he had some beef with Ben Cassar's company. Refused to work with him, she'd said. Was that because Cassar had skipped out on a $67,000 debt?

Sure, that was a lot of money, and I could totally see

why Nick would be bitter. Particularly if he was now finding it hard to get work because of it—and there was Ben, driving around town in his Lamborghini, living it up in his beautiful mansion with his beautiful wife, apparently untouched by the experience. But would he be bitter enough to kill?

The Deed of Company Arrangement had been signed nearly a year ago. That was a long time to nurse a grudge. If Nick was the killer, why had he waited so long to strike?

Listen to yourself, Charlie. "If Nick was the killer." Why was I sitting here, waiting for Andrea and Nick to appear so I could cross the road and "happen" to bump into them, as if I was an undercover cop? It wasn't as though I was going to crack the case—that was Detective McGovern's job. However bad his people skills, I was sure he was good at it. Useless cops didn't get promoted to detective.

I fanned my hair out, lifting it off my sweaty neck. It was another warm day, and if I sat here much longer I'd start to look like a stalker—a melted stalker, at that. At least there was a sea breeze this close to the water.

Andrea went to the gym during her lunch break most days. I guessed I was sitting here melting out of worry for her. She wasn't exactly going out with Nick, but it seemed pretty clear that she was at least interested in him. I would've hated for her to get involved, only to find out later that he was a killer. And he had been out of his seat when I'd first approached Andrea's table. He'd probably just been chatting to someone at another table—I hadn't seen where he'd been—but he might have had an opportunity to poison Ben's meal.

Admittedly, he hadn't seemed like a killer, in my brief introduction to him, and I was inclined to like anyone who shared my interest in photography, but after my recent experiences I didn't have the same confidence in my own judgement that I'd once had. Maybe I was too trusting—no, make that I was *definitely* too trusting. I tended to assume the best about people until they proved themselves undeserving of trust.

Did that make me like Marianne from *Sense and Sensibility*? She was the dreamy, trusting sister who got her heart broken by the guy who looked good on the outside but who was rotten to the core. Was I too influenced by outer appearances, instead of looking deeper? Would Nick turn out to be as fickle as Marianne's great love Willoughby? I owed it to Andrea to dig a little deeper.

I glanced at my watch. Nearly half past one. Andrea was due back at the library soon—I guessed today wasn't one of the days they were having coffee after their workout. Maybe they only did that on the weekends.

The automatic doors slid open, revealing an Andrea glowing with good health, eyes on her phone screen. I jumped up before she could see me and realise I'd been waiting, and stepped out between two parked cars to cross the road.

"Andrea!" I called.

She looked up and smiled as I joined her on the footpath. "Hello there! What are you doing here? Going to join the gym?"

"Not me. I'm more of a 'slow walks along the beach' kind of girl. The gym is too much like hard work."

"It would do you good." She flicked her hair, still damp from the shower, over one shoulder. She smelled of soap and apple-y shampoo, fresh and clean. "Get your blood pumping."

"Are you calling me sluggish?"

"We-ell, now you mention it ..." She grinned. "I heard that dog was running rings around you on the beach on Saturday at the wedding."

I laughed. "Fitness has nothing to do with it. That dog would run rings around anyone. He has an endless supply of energy—until he doesn't. It's either *go go go* full bore or dead stop with him." I glanced behind her, but the doors remained closed. "How was your workout?"

"Yoga today, so not so much of a workout. But I'm feeling very zen. Are you expecting someone?"

I glanced back at her a little guiltily. "No. I was just wondering if Nick was around. You said you often saw him at the gym."

"It's not as though we arrange to meet up or anything," she said. "We just keep similar schedules. I think he was in the weights room when I arrived but I didn't speak to him. We'll probably grab a coffee on Friday afternoon—that's my afternoon off. Every other day I have to rush back to work."

The automatic doors slid open again, releasing a hiss of cool air that smelled faintly of chlorine and sweat, and the man in question stepped out, gym bag over his shoulder and damp T-shirt stuck to his sweaty chest. Clearly he hadn't taken time for a shower.

He checked on the top step, surprised to see us

standing there in the street. "Hello, ladies. Charlie, isn't it?"

"That's right. How are you, Nick?" Now that I had him here, the impossibility of my task loomed before me. How on earth was I going to get him to open up about his dealings with Ben Cassar to a virtual stranger?

"Yeah, good, thanks." He glanced at Andrea. "Andrea told me you were still there when they took Troy away on Saturday night."

Well, that was a help. If he wanted to talk about the case, I wasn't going to discourage him.

"Yes, it was a long night."

"I'd love to chat," Andrea said, glancing at her watch, "but I've got to run. I'm due back at the library in five minutes."

"No worries. I'll catch you later." I waved as she headed off at a brisk walk, then turned back to Nick. "Have you got time for a coffee? I can tell you all about it."

"Sure."

He fell into step beside me as we walked down the hill towards the water. There were a couple of cafés here, and more down at the marina. I headed for one I'd tried before, right at the water's edge. The view was unbeatable, and the coffee was to die for, rich and smooth.

Waterloo Bay Marina had a modern, if small, shopping complex—several ritzy clothing stores, a couple of souvenir shops, and a handful of restaurants and cafés. There was an ice cream parlour next to the café I stopped at. I'd avoided it so far because the ice cream was wickedly expensive, but they had flavours I'd never even heard of. One of these days I'd have to try it.

We took a seat in the shaded outdoor area of the café. Deep green water sparkled in the sun only metres away, and boats bobbed at anchor in the marina, their masts forming a steel forest. Some of the boats were monsters, and I could only imagine how wealthy you would have to be to own one. Bet none of those guys were baulking at spending ten bucks on an ice cream cone.

"It's so pretty here," I said, leaning back in my chair once we'd ordered. It was a beautiful day, and Waterloo Bay was looking picture-perfect. There were a couple of larger boats out in the middle of the bay—probably dolphin-watching cruises—but from here they were small white shapes surrounded by blue sea and clear blue sky.

"Very photogenic. Makes me wish I still had all my darkroom gear sometimes."

"You got rid of it when you went digital?"

"Actually someone stole most of it. I had it stored at Mum and Dad's, and last year when they were in New Zealand, someone hit their house. They must have brought a truck, because they cleaned out anything that looked even remotely valuable. TVs, laptops, jewellery, as well as a bunch of junk like my darkroom equipment. Joke's on them because that stuff isn't worth anything these days." He shrugged. "Everyone's gone digital."

I wondered if he'd had any cyanide among his developing chemicals, but didn't bother asking. If he were a killer he'd only lie about it. I stared out over the bay. "It's hard to believe that someone could be murdered in a place like this."

"People are people everywhere," Nick said, in an unconscious echo of Ella the day before. "And there are some people that are just asking for it."

"Asking to be murdered? Why do you say that?"

"It's no secret what kind of man Cassar was. He collected enemies the way other people collect stamps. So what happened with Troy?"

"They found his bag with his insulin and needles and Detective McGovern insisted he come down to the station for further questioning."

"That McGovern's like a terrier with a bone. He'll keep gnawing away at Troy until he gets what he wants." He stopped speaking as the waitress delivered our coffees. When she'd gone, he added, "But I reckon he's barking up the wrong tree."

"Oh? You have a theory?"

He shrugged. "It's got to be the wife, hasn't it? I saw her having lunch down at the surf club with a new guy last week. Seemed very chummy, if you know what I mean. I reckon she'd finally decided to move on and didn't want to spend years fighting over money in the divorce courts."

"She seems to have a lot of money," I said, thinking of the magnificent house on the hill. "I can see how it might be tempting. But presumably Detective McGovern will be looking at her, too."

"He's thorough, I'll give him that. What did he ask you?"

"It was pretty standard stuff." I recounted my interview with the detective, then told him about Delia's investigation in the kitchen with the chef and the waiters.

"Interesting." He added sugar to his coffee and stirred thoughtfully. "Can't imagine Pete Bunning took that well. He's so precious about his food you'd think he was running an exclusive restaurant in Paris."

"I think he was just too shocked. Everyone was—especially Ella. She was one of the waitresses that night. She completely fell apart when she heard the news."

He shook his head. "I don't know what she ever saw in Cassar. She was head over heels for him."

"I didn't know Ben at all—was he particularly charismatic? He seemed to be the centre of attention at his table at the wedding."

"I suppose you could call it that," he said darkly. "He was pretty full of himself. But people did seem to like him, at least until they got to know him better. He knew how to turn on the charm when it suited him."

He toyed with the handle of his cup, turning it this way and that.

"How well did you know him?"

"Not well enough, as it turned out. I thought we were mates, but he suckered me."

"Why? What happened?"

He took a sip, then set his cup down with a sigh. "I was working for him—sub-contracting, but basically working for him. He had this big development going on at Waterloo Bay, and there wasn't a lot of other work around, so I was full time with Cassar Building for about six months. At first everything was fine, but then he started getting slow paying my invoices. I spoke to him about it and he was all apologetic, promised me it was just a temporary cashflow problem. So I kept going. I mean, what else could I do? If I wanted to work locally, he was the only game in town."

"And you didn't want to travel for work?"

"I guess it was stupid, in hindsight." He shrugged. "There's plenty of work in Newcastle, but that's an hour each way, and I like the lifestyle here. Going for a surf in the morning before work, done for the day by two or three and hitting the gym. I was living the dream, you know?"

"So I'm guessing the cashflow problem wasn't temporary?"

"Who knows what the truth is? He seemed to have plenty of cash for buying Ella expensive jewellery and taking her to restaurants. But he got later and later with the payments, and then he stopped taking my calls. Before I knew it, he owed me more than sixty grand."

Sixty-seven, to be exact, but I pretended to be surprised. "Wow. That's a lot. So what did you do?"

"I turned up at his house, since he wouldn't take my calls anymore, and demanded payment. I had bills to pay —I was behind on the rent, and I'd used all my savings. He promised me it was all getting sorted out and I'd get my money soon. Opened up his wallet and offered me a couple of hundred 'just to tide me over'. Like a fool, I said no. It felt too much like taking charity, as if I'd come begging for handouts. I should have taken the lot. That wallet was full of fifties, and it was all other people's money that he'd scammed." He drained his cup and set it back on the saucer with a clatter. "Next thing I knew, that accounting firm was calling a meeting of his creditors."

"That was Green and Fenwick?"

"You know about this?"

"Sarah told me. He never finished building their house."

"Ah. There were a lot of angry people at that first meeting. It was a bit of a shock to realise the extent of the problem. It wasn't just a few tradies he owed money to, it was more like half the town. We got seven cents in the dollar out of that stupid Deed of Arrangement, and he kept his business as though nothing had happened." His mouth twisted. "I shouldn't talk about this. It just makes me angry all over again."

Angry enough to kill? I studied his face as he gazed out across the water. He was frowning, and there was a hard glint in his eyes. Andrea liked him—but how well did she know him? Even murderers could take a woman out to coffee and be nice to them.

"Why did you agree to the Deed if the payout was so small?"

"Because the alternative was getting nothing. He had hardly any money left, and the bank took what there was. The bank was a 'secured creditor'." He made air quotes with his fingers. "Apparently that means they get their debts paid out and the rest of us get the scraps that are left."

"But he still had that big house, and the Lamborghini —couldn't you sue for the rest?"

"He was too cunning. All that was in his wife's name, and she had no connection to the company. Cassar himself owned the clothes on his back and nothing much else. There were no assets to go after. The accountants explained all this at the meeting. They said the Deed was our only chance to get at least something of what we were owed. And if we signed it, we agreed not to take any further legal action."

"So your hands were tied."

"Pretty much. So I got my four grand, borrowed money from my parents to pay my bills, and moved back in with them. I've got my truck and my tools, and that's about it. Meanwhile Cassar's wife starts up a new company, employs Cassar, and it's business as usual. Cassar's driving around town in his flashy car, acting like nothing ever happened."

"I can understand you being furious."

He folded his arms and gave me a level look. "Furious doesn't begin to cover it. I'd like to shake the hand of whoever poisoned him."

"I imagine a few of his creditors would feel the same."

He snorted. "I reckon they'll be lining up to spit on his grave. But poison was too easy. If I'd done it, I would have gouged his heart out with a trowel. Made sure he suffered before he died."

CHAPTER 13

NEXT MORNING WAS THURSDAY AND MY MEETING WITH WILL. I changed my mind three times about what to wear, and ended up throwing on a plain white T-shirt and faded blue denim shorts. Then I decided that looked too bland and added a hot pink necklace to brighten it up.

Not that it mattered how I looked. I wasn't dressing up —or down—for Will anymore. He'd always liked me in more conservative, classy clothes, which was what I'd worn to the office. My wardrobe had been full of pencil skirts and soft silken shirts, with jackets in half a dozen different colours, all some variation on shades of blue or grey.

Now I was dressing for me, for comfort in the heat and in clothes that suited my new life. And if the frayed hem on the shorts made him shudder, all the better.

There was no sign of Rufus as I left the house. I'd gotten used to having him along on almost all my walks and I missed him trotting along at my side, his tail waving like a plumed flag. He was good company—better than Will was likely to be. I was dreading this meeting.

I'd left early, hoping to arrive at the café first, but Will was already there. His bright red hair was easy to spot in a crowd. He was seated at one of the outdoor tables with a coffee in front of him and another opposite. I was so busy staring at him that I almost walked straight into Gail Cassar.

"Did you hear McGovern's called Ella back in for questioning?" she asked without even a hello. "Didn't I tell you it was her?"

Questioning wasn't the same as proof. I smiled awkwardly at the man with her. He was a little older than her, with those silver streaks at his temples that people always called "distinguished" on men and "aging" on women.

"I saw Ella just after I left your place, actually." Might as well see what I could get out of her since she was here. "She told me that Ben was planning to leave you for her."

Gail exchanged glances with her companion, then burst out laughing. "Oh, honey. I've lost count of how many women he's said that to. If she believed him she's an even bigger fool than I thought. Trust me, he was ready to dump her. I can always tell. And I bet she knew it too, and she didn't like it one bit. This is revenge, plain and simple. McGovern needs to stop wasting time on Troy Chapman."

"Why don't you think Troy did it? There was some bad blood between them."

"You saw him at the wedding—he's the kind of person who gets a thought in his head and acts on it straight away. He lost his house nearly a year ago. You think he would have waited this long to do something about it? But Ella was sacked last week. Timing is everything." She glanced at her watch then tipped her head at her companion. "And speaking of which ..."

"Yes. We'd better go," he said.

"Don't waste your sympathy on Miss Giordano," she said to me as she brushed past. "She's not the victim here."

I watched her go, the man following close behind. Was he the guy Nick had seen her with before? He hadn't acted like a lover, but perhaps they were being discreet. Her husband had only been dead a few days.

I shook my head and went to join Will. He got up, smiling, as I approached, looking as though he meant to kiss me hello. I wasn't having that, so I pulled out the empty seat and plopped into it, leaving him hovering awkwardly by the table.

"I got you a latte with two sugars, just the way you like it," he said as he resumed his seat.

He'd often ordered for me when we were together. Not just coffees, either, but whole meals sometimes if he was taking me to one of his favourite restaurants. I used to think it was charming, but now I found it annoying. Far from being a sign of his thoughtfulness, it felt more like an attempt to manage everything and impose his will on me.

Maybe that was too much meaning to assign to a simple coffee, but I called the waiter over anyway and ordered an iced chocolate.

"It's too hot this morning for coffee," I said to him.

"It's going to be a warm one," he agreed, as he entered my order on his iPad. "Your iced chocolate won't be a minute."

"Thanks. Um ... did you see that woman in the white pants suit who just left?"

"You mean Gail Cassar?"

"Yes. Do you know who that guy with her was?"

"I don't know his name, but I've seen him around before. I think he's married to her cousin, the one who lives in Newcastle."

"Ah. Thanks." Not a new lover, then. So much for Nick's theory.

The waiter went inside and Will leaned forward, eager to recapture my attention. "Did you walk all the way here?" He made it sound like a two-hour trek instead of a ten-minute walk. "Why didn't you drive?"

"It's a nice day for a walk." I wasn't going to tell him I was temporarily car-less. That would mean talking about the accident and the whole murder thing that had caused it—and that was way more conversation than I planned on having with Will. He had until I finished my drink, and then I was done. "So, why did we need to have this meeting? And why are you here in Sunny Bay anyway?"

"I needed some time off work, so I thought I'd come up and see my favourite girl."

I took a deep breath, hating this already. He made it sound like a casual decision, but I knew him too well. Will did nothing without a plan. Even his plans had plans. And I didn't want to be the subject of any more plans of his.

He was giving me that rueful smile that had always got

him out of trouble with me before. But this wasn't a matter of double-booking an event, or having to work late when he'd promised to come home and spend the evening with me.

"I'm not your anything girl anymore," I said. "You chose Amy. Why don't you spend your break hanging out with her?"

"Amy and I aren't together."

"Wow, that was fast."

"We weren't ever together," he said, almost impatiently.

"No, you were supposedly with me—you were just banging her on the side."

"I don't want to talk about Amy."

"Neither do I, but you made it about her when you slept with her three months before our wedding."

His gaze slid to the side, and I got that same sinking feeling in my gut that I'd had when I'd walked in on them together.

"Right. I guess you were sleeping with her before that. That was just the time I actually caught you at it." Man, I'd thought I was over this, but the rage and hurt boiled up all over again, and my vision blurred with angry tears. "How long was it going on? Weeks? Months? How many of those late-night work functions were work and how many were an excuse to meet up with Amy?"

"Babe, don't cry—"

"Don't call me that."

The waiter came back with my iced chocolate, and I glared at Will over the rim of the glass as I took a hasty sip.

"You have cream on your nose," he said.

I wiped it off with a paper napkin from the dispenser, then blew my nose on the napkin, too. I hated that I cried so easily, but it didn't mean I was weak or soft. I was *angry*, not sad.

"I'm sorry that I hurt you," he said. "But it wasn't months. A few weeks, that's all. It was madness. I don't know what came over me. She dropped in one night, when you were away for the weekend visiting Evie, and we got talking, had a few drinks. A few too many drinks. Then she starts crying and saying how unhappy she is ... and you know what a sucker I am for a woman in tears. I gave her a hug, and then suddenly we were kissing ... I never meant for anything to happen."

He was giving me such a serious face, as if he could compel me to believe him by sheer willpower alone. No sign of the rueful little grin anymore.

"And all of a sudden you were comforting her with your penis."

A woman walking past gave me a startled look, and Will shifted uncomfortably in his seat. "Look, I know there's no excuse—"

"You're right about that."

"—but you and I were so busy. Work was crazy for both of us, plus you were so caught up in wedding plans, it was like we were just room-mates. I hardly saw you; there was no excitement in our lives. I didn't feel as though you needed me at all."

"So you're saying it's *my* fault that you slept with

someone else?" Only Will could turn things on their heads like that.

"No, of course not." He made an impatient noise. "This is all coming out wrong."

You could say that again. Not that there was any right way that would magically make me fall back into his arms. I took another sip of my iced chocolate, watching him flail without any desire to throw him a lifeline.

"Let me make it up to you," he said. "We can start all over again. And this time I'll romance you the way you deserve."

I couldn't help a snort of disbelief. "This from the man who said Valentine's Day was a stupid commercial thing made up by florists and card companies? You don't have a romantic bone in your body. You said people who really love each other don't need all that symbolic garbage. Garbage, that's what you called it. I distinctly remember it." I remembered it because I'd been hurt, after getting him a thoughtful gift for our first Valentine's Day together, to be told I'd wasted my money on being a slave to capitalism.

"Don't throw my past mistakes in my face! I was wrong. I see that now. People need to know that you care. *You* need to know I care. We had something special and I screwed it up, and that's on me, but I'm going to fix it." He reached across the table for my hand, but I was too quick for him and tucked both hands in my lap. After a moment's pause, he soldiered on. "I'll prove my love, any way you want. Candlelight dinners, luxury weekends away. You're the centre of my world, Charlie, and it's time I showed you that."

"I don't want to be shown." I missed the life I'd thought I had and the future I'd dreamed of. I even missed Will, hurt and angry with him as I was. He'd been part of my life for so long. He was as familiar to me as my own skin. But what was the point of rehashing it all yet again? Talking about it only scraped the scab off a wound that had barely begun to heal. "I want you to leave me alone. This is over, Will. *We're* over, and all the candlelight dinners in the world can't change that. You destroyed my trust in you, and we can't get back what we had."

"Then let's build something better. I know I wasn't always the best boyfriend. I took you for granted. I'm not going to make that mistake again."

"It was a little more than taking me for granted," I said snappily. I wasn't letting him get away with rewriting our history into something more palatable for him. "You slept with my best friend and lied to me about it. Repeatedly. I don't think there's any building something better after that."

"Just give me a chance." His eyes were earnest, pleading almost. "I know I did something terrible. Some people might say unforgiveable. But I know how big your heart is, Charlie. If anyone could forgive me, it's you. Forget Amy. I have."

Was *I know how big your heart is* just code for *I know you're a sucker, Charlie*? I sure felt like a sucker, because those pleading eyes were drawing me in.

You don't want this, I told myself firmly. It was easy for him to say, *forget Amy*. Not quite as easy for me to do, with the image of them tangled together in the bed burnt into my brain.

"There's more to it than that," I said. "Maybe Amy was just a symptom, but there must have been something seriously wrong for her to even become an option. And you never said anything. You didn't say you were unhappy. I had no idea there was even a problem until I walked in on the two of you."

"I wasn't unhappy," he insisted. "It was just a moment of madness, like I said."

"A moment that lasted for weeks, apparently."

"You're right, you're right. It was more than a moment. I don't know what I was thinking. She just kind of took over and I went along with everything. She's a go-getter. It's hard to say no to someone like that."

"She's a go-getter," I repeated, dumbfounded. He made it sound like she'd made some smart career move.

"Yeah. She's completely different to you."

"Because I don't sleep with other people's fiancés."

"No, because you're a dreamer, and I love that about you."

Funny, I'd never thought Will had much time for dreamers. He was practical, focused on facts and figures. In fact, just the type to admire someone like Amy, who'd been running her own successful online business for years. Was I the Marianne in this situation, and Amy was practical Elinor? Was I the one full of ridiculous romantic notions of what a relationship should be, while Will and Amy saw things as they were?

If that was the case, I wasn't interested in their kind of relationship.

"You and Amy destroyed the dreams I had," I told him. "And now I have new ones."

"I have new ones, too," he said. "But they all include you. I want you back, Charlie, you and your dreams. We can build a new life together."

I pushed back from the table and stood up. My iced chocolate was still half full, but I'd had enough of this conversation.

"I *have* built a new life, and I don't want you in it. It's over, Will. Please accept that."

"You don't mean that, Charlie."

"Yes, I do." I walked away, praying he didn't follow.

"I'll make you change your mind," he called after me.

My heart sank. I seriously doubted that he could, but I had a feeling I wasn't going to enjoy his attempts.

CHAPTER 14

"When is your new car coming?" Aunt Evie asked as we lugged my groceries in from her car.

She was puffing a little and I immediately felt guilty. "Aunt Evie, I told you, I can carry these. Give me that bag! It's too heavy for you."

"Rubbish!" she said, clinging to the bag stubbornly and whisking past me into the kitchen, where she deposited it triumphantly on the bench. "I'm perfectly capable of carrying a few bags of groceries. I daresay I'm fitter than you are."

"I feel bad enough getting you to drive me to the supermarket without having you lumping bags as well. Would you *please* leave the rest for me?"

"It's no trouble," she said. "I have to get my own groceries anyway. May as well take you with me. Besides, it's nice to spend some time together."

"Yes, but we could spend time together without manual labour," I said, dumping the last bag on the bench.

"Anyway, the insurance company says the car will be delivered next week, so this should be the last time I have to impose on you."

"It's not imposing, you silly child." She rubbed her knuckles down my cheek in a quick caress. "Families help each other out."

I smiled at her. "Well, why don't you help out by making some tea and leave me to put these away?"

She opened the cupboard where I kept the teabags. "I suppose I could," she said a little grudgingly. "I could probably just about manage that in my feeble state."

Oh, dear, I had put my foot in it. She hated being treated like an old lady. "I know you're a very capable woman, Aunt Evie. I just want to look after you, the way you've always looked after me."

"Hmph. Earl Grey or peppermint?"

"Peppermint, please."

I busied myself putting away the groceries, then I got out a plate for the tarts I'd picked up at the bakery in Sunny Bay earlier. They made the most delicious citrus tarts so I'd bought a couple of those, plus the neenish tarts that Aunt Evie loved. They were too sickly sweet for me, but hopefully, she would accept them as a peace offering.

The boiling water bubbled away, then the kettle clicked off and Aunt Evie poured hot water into two mugs. "I really should get you a proper teapot. I swear tea tastes better from a pot than when it's made with a tea bag."

"You're such a tea snob," I said teasingly. "Teabags are so much quicker."

"That's the trouble with you young people," she said

as she carried the mugs to my little dining table. "You always want everything now. Instant gratification! Some things are worth waiting for, like a nice brew from a well-seasoned pot." She sat down and took a sip from her mug. "And I prefer the term *connoisseur* to *tea snob*, thank you very much."

I brought the plate with the tarts on it to the table and sat opposite her. Her smile told me that I was forgiven.

Aunt Evie eyed the bouquet of roses on the kitchen bench over the rim of her mug. It had come this morning before I left to see Will, and I hadn't bothered doing anything with it yet.

"I see Will is still attempting to crawl back into your good graces. Why haven't you spoken to him yet?"

"I have, actually. Obviously he didn't take the message on board."

"Ah. Well, you tried. If he wants to support the local florist shop singlehandedly, I suppose that's his business. Stupid man. Doesn't he realise that annoying you is no way to win you back?"

"Apparently not. He can be very stubborn when he sets his mind on something."

"Well, I'm proud of you for confronting him about it. It couldn't have been easy. I imagine he didn't take it well?"

I grimaced at my tea. "No, not well."

To Aunt Evie's credit, she didn't press for more information, though I knew perfectly well she was bursting to hear every gory detail. She bit into one of the neenish tarts and gave a small sigh of contentment.

"These are really good." She brandished the disgusting

cream-filled thing with its garish pink and brown icing at me. "I love a good neenish tart. Did you get them from Jenny's Bakery?"

"Yeah. I picked them up on my way back from seeing Will. The beach was pretty crowded this morning."

"I went for a walk on the beach this morning, too. I didn't see you. What time were you there?"

"I think I left about ten-thirty."

She rolled her eyes. "Ten-thirty! Half the day's gone by then. I was down there before seven. I like to get my walk in before it gets too hot. I saw Marco Lombardi down there, too. He'd just come back in from surfing. They must be back from their honeymoon."

I bit into my citrus tart and nearly moaned with delight. The tang of the lemon, the crumble of the pastry —it was perfect. "Yeah, Sarah said they were only away for a few days," I said when I could speak again.

"Has Molly contacted you about the photos yet?"

"No. At least, I don't think so. I haven't checked my emails yet this morning." I jumped up and went to retrieve my laptop from the coffee table in the lounge room. "Excuse me for a moment while I check."

"See? That's what I mean. Instant gratification," she grumbled, but I could tell from her grin that she was only teasing.

"No," I said after a moment. "No email from Molly."

"She probably hasn't had a chance to do anything yet if they only just got back. You said you sent her the link to the gallery?"

"Yes, as soon as I had all the photos loaded."

"Could you show me? I'd love to see them."

"Of course." I shifted to the chair next to her and opened up the wedding gallery, setting it up as a slideshow to scroll slowly through the photos. "There's a lot in here that you probably won't be interested in. Photos of each table and so on. Do you want to just look at the pretty shots of the bridal party on the beach?"

"No, I want to see everything." She slanted a smile at me. "I want to see how talented my clever niece is. You know, I haven't seen any of your work yet except for that beautiful photo of Heidi's children she's got up on the wall of her shop."

"Just warning you—there are a ton of photos."

"In that case, perhaps you'd better make me another tea." She pushed her empty cup toward me as the first photos of Molly getting ready scrolled across the screen. "Of course, if you had a teapot, you could just pour a second cup without having to do any more work."

I grinned as I took both empty cups to the kitchen and set the kettle boiling again. "Such a nagger."

"Just pointing out the truth. Is it my fault if you find it inconvenient?"

When I came back to the table with the two cups of tea, Aunt Evie was up to the photos in the water. Marco, pants rolled to the knees, laughed at the camera as he swung a giggling Molly around, the sky bright blue behind them.

"You got some really lovely shots of the wedding ceremony," she said. "The way Marco looked at her when she slid the ring on his finger—it was so precious. It almost brought a tear to my eye."

"Mine too."

She shot me a sympathetic glance. "This must have been hard for you, so close to your own cancelled wedding. Though I hope you'll come to see this as a lucky escape one day. That Will is bad news."

I took a sip of my tea. Why could I agree that Will was bad news, yet still mourn the loss of the future we'd been looking forward to together? Was I just a ridiculously romantic Marianne?

"Oh, it's nothing to do with that," I assured her. That wasn't the whole truth, but it was enough of the truth for now. "I always cry at weddings."

"Do you?" She got a faraway look in her eye. "Your mother was just the same. Hopelessly emotional. Used to blub like a baby at weddings. Christenings, too. Basically anything that involved any emotion at all. She wore her heart on her sleeve. Anyway." She cleared her throat and turned back to the screen. "These photos are lovely."

She exclaimed over the cuteness of the flower girls and admired everything from the flowers to the weather to the composition of the photos and the beauty of the bride. We spent a very pleasant half-hour drinking tea, eating tarts, and admiring my work. I'll admit, it gave me a warm glow to see the photos through Aunt Evie's eyes. It was nice to have such unstinting praise for my efforts.

"Ooh," she said, when we had moved on to the reception and the photos of the groupings at each table. "Is that Ben Cassar? How do you stop this thing?"

I stopped the slideshow and clicked back to the photo of Ben Cassar's table. There he was, with his big, beaming *I'm the king of the world* smile, with Gail beside him, as cold and unresponsive as a statue in her silly feathered hat. Her mouth was making a smiling motion, but you could tell her heart wasn't in it. She was even still leaning slightly away from her husband.

"There you go."

"Oh, look at Neville Botham. I didn't realise he'd been invited. He scrubbed up all right for the occasion, didn't he?"

I smiled at the dapper old man in his red bow tie on Ben's other side. "He seemed like a sweetheart. I gather you know him, then?"

"Of course I know him. He lives at Sunrise Lodge. Not near me, but I see him out and about. He takes a walk every day and we often chat about the gardens."

"I liked him."

"It's hard to believe that the poor man was dead not long after this was taken," Aunt Evie mused, staring at Ben.

"I wonder if his killer is in this photo."

Aunt Evie studied the picture with renewed interest. "I bet it was his wife. She doesn't look too happy with him, does she?"

"It seems to be most people's favourite theory," I said, thinking of Sarah and Ella. "Admittedly, it would have been easy for her to poison his meal or drink, since she's sitting right next to him."

"That's true," Aunt Evie said thoughtfully. "It certainly

wouldn't have been Neville and it would have been too obvious for anyone else to reach over and do it—unless they did it when they were moving around getting set up for the photo. Mrs Sarno is standing right behind him—could she have done it?"

I shrugged, studying the grey-haired matron behind Ben. "Your guess is as good as mine. Do you know her?"

"Not well, but I know she volunteers at Vinnies every Wednesday. A good Catholic."

"Being a good Catholic doesn't mean a person can't also commit a crime, but what motive would she have?"

"I have no idea. As far as I know, she doesn't even know Ben Cassar. Didn't know, I suppose I should say. Perhaps it wasn't someone at the table at all. It might have been one of the waiters or the kitchen staff."

"I thought you said Peter Bunning would never do something like that?"

"No, of course he wouldn't. But he wasn't the only one working in the kitchen, was he?"

I stared at the photo. Something was niggling at me about it, but I couldn't put my finger on it. "I can't see how the kitchen staff could have managed it unless they were in league with one of the waiters. Those meals were set down pretty much at random and they all looked the same."

"Well, not at random," Aunt Evie objected. "They alternate them, don't they? They always have at functions I've been to, at least."

"You know what I mean. Each waiter took an armful—three or four plates at a time—and the chefs had no idea which plates would go to which tables, much less to which person." I looked at the meals on the table in front of Gail and Ben and Neville Botham and a thrill of excitement ran through me. Now I could see what had been bothering me about the photo. "Hang on a minute. Ben has the beef in front of him—but so has Gail."

The way the photo was angled, we could see Gail, Ben, and Neville's meals clearly, plus half of Neville's neighbour's meal. Gail and Ben both had beef dinners in front of them and Neville and his neighbour both had chicken.

Aunt Evie peered more closely at the photo. "Did the waiters get it wrong?"

"I doubt it. I bet you anything Ben swapped with Neville." It made perfect sense to me. Most men seemed to prefer red meat to white. But Ben had missed out and been given the chicken in the alternating order. The beef meal had gone to his wife and, even if Ben had had the courage to ask her to swap with him, I bet she would have said no just to spite him.

"And Neville would have said yes. He's the most agreeable thing. Chicken probably would have been easier on his teeth than beef anyway."

"Right." That made sense. Each of them would have been happy with the trade. Then I frowned. "But that means the murderer must have only had a tiny window of opportunity to put the poison on Ben's meal. Only the time between when he swapped with Neville and they all started eating. It could have only been seconds."

"It makes Gail look more likely as the killer, doesn't it?

She's sitting there right next to him. It would be easier for her than anyone else."

"Unless ..." I thought back to the bustle and busy-ness of the wedding reception. What if the poison had been added to the meal somewhere in its transit from the kitchen to the table? Half of the people at the table had been out of their seats, moving into position for the photo as the waiters weaved their dance around the table, depositing meals. Jimmy, the tall young waiter, had nearly dropped one of the plates, obviously not as well versed in the fine art of carrying multiple meals at a time as the others. And plenty of other people had been out of their seats, moving around, including Nick. I'd been jostled a couple of times by people squeezing past in the spaces between tables. There could have been a dozen people who'd had the opportunity to tip a little something extra onto a plate as it went past on a waiter's arm.

But that was still such a lottery. No guarantee where the poisoned plate would finish up. Whoever had done it must have waited until they saw the pattern, until they could predict which plate would end up in which spot. Then it would only be a matter of timing their walk past the waiter.

I stared at Neville Botham's beaming face on the screen. The poisoned meal had ended up in front of him. Was he the one who was supposed to die?

CHAPTER 15

At Aunt Evie's urging, I rang Detective McGovern as soon as she left. I felt nervous as I waited for him to answer, as if I were a criminal who'd done something wrong instead of a citizen just trying to be helpful. He had told me to ring if I thought of anything else, so here I was, ringing. He could hardly get annoyed about that.

"McGovern," he said gruffly. He sounded just as grumpy as he had the night of the wedding. Maybe grumpy was his natural state.

"Hi." I cleared my throat. "This is Charlie Carter, the photographer from Molly and Marco's wedding. You interviewed me about Ben Cassar's death."

"I know who you are." He sounded impatient. Apparently he *could* get annoyed about concerned citizens doing their civic duty. "What can I do for you?"

"You said to ring if I thought of anything else. I was just looking at the group photo from Ben's table and I noticed something interesting."

"Yes?" Now he sounded bored.

I picked up the pen that lay next to my notepad on the dining table and started to fiddle with it nervously. "I noticed that the order of the meals on the table was wrong. The waiters put them down in an alternating pattern: one chicken, then one beef. But Ben and his wife both had the beef, which means he must have swapped with Mr Botham, who was sitting next to him." The silence lengthened. It felt disapproving, somehow, and I hurried on. "And I got to thinking, what if Ben wasn't supposed to die at all? What if the murderer poisoned that beef meal thinking that Mr Botham was going to eat it, and then they swapped and the wrong man died?"

"That's an interesting theory, Miss Carter," he said, in a tone that made it clear he'd never heard anything less interesting in his life, "but I don't think there's any doubt that Ben Cassar was the intended victim. We're very close at this point to making an arrest."

"Who?" I regretted it as soon as the word was out of my mouth.

"I can't tell you that, Miss Carter," he said, as patronisingly as I had expected for such a stupid question. "This is a murder investigation and I am a detective, not a gossip columnist."

Heat blossomed in my cheeks and I was glad he couldn't see me. Of course he couldn't give away that kind of information, but I'd been so surprised that the question was out of my mouth before my brain could catch up.

But he didn't have to be so insulting about it. *I am not a gossip columnist.* No, and he wasn't much of a human being, either. My first impressions of the detective had not been favourable, but I'd put his grumpiness down to the lateness of the hour. I was rapidly discovering that it went deeper than that. I took a deep breath and tried again.

"But are you sure you've got the right person? What if I'm right? Mr Botham could still be in danger." *And you could be arresting the wrong person entirely.*

"I think you're letting your imagination run away with you. Why would anyone want to kill a harmless old man like Mr Botham? He's nearly ninety and he lives in a retirement village. Did he take someone's favourite spot in the dining room and now they're gunning for him?"

More rudeness. My already low opinion of Detective McGovern was sinking through the floor.

His implication was that there were plenty of people who wanted to kill Ben Cassar, which I had already discovered for myself. It was therefore logical that he must be the intended victim, but my gut was telling me that logic wasn't the right way to look at this. While the police were distracted chasing down the multitudes of people who didn't like Ben Cassar and probably arresting an innocent person to boot, poor old Neville Botham was a sitting duck. There was nothing to stop the murderer from making another attempt. And this time getting it right. I dropped the pen and started to pace a small circle around the dining table.

"Can you at least tell me if the poison was in the meal? Or was it in his drink?" That would ease my mind. If it was in the drink and not the meal, then swapping meals made no difference and Neville Botham was out of danger.

"I'm afraid I can't share details of our investigation." The detective's voice hardened. "I heard about your brush with murder a few weeks back. I hope you don't have any ideas of being an amateur sleuth. This is not an Agatha Christie novel and I assure you we don't need any civilians butting into our investigation."

My face burned but I pushed on. "I'm not butting in, I'm trying to help." He didn't need to be so rude about it. "You said to ring if I thought of anything. I'm genuinely concerned about Mr Botham's safety."

"I meant to ring if you thought of any additional facts, Miss Carter. Not if you intended to waste my time with wild speculation. Thank you for your call."

He hung up without saying goodbye and I stared at my phone in indignation for a moment. He was being a jerk—and worse than that, he was ignoring what could be a crucial new piece of evidence. Clearly he'd already made up his mind about the identity of the murderer and didn't want to hear anything that challenged his tidy little solution to the case. Did he get a bonus for solving them fast?

That was a little catty, maybe, but I wasn't feeling very kindly disposed to Detective McGovern. I couldn't help comparing his style to Curtis's. Admittedly Curtis wasn't a detective, but he was everything you could want in a police officer—kind, concerned, and quietly competent.

Of course, it didn't hurt that he was also pretty easy on the eye. If the police force ever decided to do one of those calendars where the officers took off their shirts and posed for charity, Curtis would be my pick for the cover. I'd never seen him without his shirt on, of course, but I could tell there were muscles under there. And that smile! I'd always had a thing for dimples.

I gave myself a mental shake. Curtis might be the best-looking guy in Sunny Bay, but I had no business getting lost in daydreaming about his charms. I was hardly in a place to even be thinking about a new romance, with the tatters of my old one still hanging around me like a shroud, and Will determined, as usual, not to take no for an answer.

My life was far too complicated right now. The photo of Ben Cassar's table at the wedding was still up on my screen, and I looked at Neville Botham's beaming face and felt my stomach clench with anxiety. My romantic problems meant very little when it seemed horribly likely to me that someone was biding their time, just waiting for a chance to kill that sweet old man. And Detective McGovern didn't even want to know about it. He was too busy trying to arrest Troy or Ella or even Gail for a crime they didn't commit.

Someone had to fix this mess, and it looked like that someone was me.

CHAPTER 16

"Oh my gosh, those photos are to die for!"

Molly had been gushing in my ear for the last ten minutes about how much she loved the wedding photos and I had to admit, it was doing my ego a world of good. I hadn't even had to ask her for a testimonial—she had offered.

"And besides, hon, I've told, like, fifty people already. I think you'll be getting a call from Debbie in the office soon to book you for her own wedding."

"That's great! I'm so glad you like them."

"Like them? I love them! I don't know how I'm going to stop myself from ordering every single one. And blowups of all those gorgeous shots on the beach. I'm so happy. They're everything I dreamed of."

It was a nice note in my day, which had started, as usual, with Steve ringing the doorbell, another enormous bouquet in his arms.

"I've gotta hand it to this guy, he's persistent," he said,

as he handed them over, then left with a jaunty, "see you tomorrow".

Will was indeed persistent, but I couldn't see that as a plus in my current circumstances. I was on my way to Sunrise Lodge, carrying those same flowers, and let me tell you, they got awfully heavy after a while when you were walking. By the time I had made it to the top of the hill where Sunrise Lodge perched on its headland overlooking the blue sweep of the bay, I was puffing and my arms felt like lead.

"More flowers?" Aunt Evie said with a grimace as she opened the front door to me. "I wish he'd take the hint."

She held the door wide and I staggered in and dumped them on her dining table, very glad to relieve myself of my burden. I flopped into one of the chairs, grateful for a rest.

"You're sweating," Aunt Evie said.

"It's hot out there."

"Well, you're going to get fit trekking up here every day with an enormous flower arrangement. When did you say your car is being delivered?"

"Next week. But I don't think they're delivering it. I'll have to go down to Newcastle to pick it up."

"Cup of tea?" She moved towards the kettle with one eyebrow raised. Aunt Evie never needed much encouragement to take a tea break.

"No, thanks. I'm actually here on a mission today."

"Oh?"

"I want to talk to Neville Botham."

"Ah." She pulled out the seat opposite me, her eyes

alight with interest. "Did you ring the detective yesterday? What did he say?"

"He basically told me to get lost. He says they're very close to making an arrest—I hope it's not Troy—and he refused to even entertain the idea that Ben Cassar wasn't the intended victim."

"Typical man." She dismissed Detective McGovern with a roll of her eyes. "They get tunnel vision—can't stand to be diverted from whatever they're focused on."

"Yes. Exhibit A: Will." Every flower arrangement was only making me more and more determined not to have anything further to do with him. At least he hadn't progressed to greater efforts. After his threats of romantic gestures I had been worried. "Anyway, I was hoping you knew which unit Neville lives in."

"Oh, yes. At least, I don't know his unit number, but I can tell you how to find him. He's in the Harrington block. That's the one closest to the Maitland Drive entry." When I nodded, she went on, "He's on the ground floor, right in the back corner, near the fishpond."

"Okay, thanks. I reckon I can find him."

"Do you want me to come with you? I could introduce you."

"No, it's fine. He should remember me from the wedding."

I gave her a hug and headed off. Now that I only had my handbag to carry, walking was much more pleasant. Sunrise Lodge covered a large area and had several streets within its boundaries. I headed back the way I had come, away from the freestanding villas like Aunt Evie's to the apartment blocks at the front of the property. They all had signage out the front with their names so the Harrington wasn't hard to locate. It was a two-storey block built around a large courtyard full of shaded gardens. At the far end, as Aunt Evie had said, a fishpond nestled under the ferns, where fat carp the length of my forearm slid like orange ghosts through the cool green water.

The unit in the corner was number ninety-eight, and I gave the door three sharp raps. A long silence followed, so I knocked again, louder this time. Perhaps Neville didn't have his hearing aids in.

Just when I was deciding that he must be out, the door opened, and Neville stood there, as tiny and bent as I remembered, though today there was no red bowtie. He wore a checked shirt and a set of old-fashioned braces held up his trousers.

"A visitor! How lovely." He beamed at me through the screen door and his smile was just as bright as I recalled from the wedding. His hands shook as he fumbled with the lock to open the door for me. "Sorry to keep you waiting. It takes me a while to get the old body into gear these days."

"That's no problem." I smiled back at him. Who could resist that infectious grin of his? "I don't know if you remember me, Mr Botham. I'm Charlie Carter. I was the photographer at Molly and Marco's wedding last weekend."

Finally he had the door open and I stepped inside, following him into a room furnished in a sombre style, its old-fashioned tables and chairs dark and bulky.

"I thought I knew your face. Come in, come in, take a seat. To what do I owe the pleasure?"

He leaned heavily on a walking stick as he faltered his way across the cream carpet to a dark brown recliner. It was so large he looked like a child in its depths when he subsided into it with a sigh of relief. I took a seat on the lounge opposite him and opened my handbag.

"I have some photos for you from the wedding. I got such a lovely one of you and Molly I couldn't wait to show it to you." I had also printed the one of him with the group at the table and a couple of general shots of the bride and groom.

His hand trembled as he accepted them from me. "With personal delivery, too. What a service! How much do I owe you?"

"Oh, no, Mr Botham. It's a gift. No need to pay."

"That's very kind of you, Charlie. And please call me Neville. All my friends do." He offered me another one of those beaming smiles.

I wanted to wrap him up in cotton wool. He was like the grandfather every kid would love to have. He leafed through the photos, pausing at the one of himself with Molly. It really was a gorgeous shot, if I did say so myself. Molly had her arm around him and he was looking up at her with a grin. One of them must have said something funny just before I snapped the picture, because she was laughing too, and they looked like best mates having a wonderful time together.

"This is really beautiful." When he looked up there were tears in his eyes. "Wasn't she a gorgeous bride? I watched her grow up, you know. We used to live next door to the Simpsons, me and Joyce. Those girls used to be in and out of our house all the time. It's hard to believe little Molly is all grown up now."

"How long have you lived here?" I asked.

"Nearly three years now. The house got too much for me. I was lonely, too, racketing around in that big old house on my own. There didn't seem much point staying without Joyce." A shadow crossed his face as he spoke of his wife, then cleared. He smiled again, his face settling into its usual happy lines. "This is a great place for an old bloke like me. Lots of company."

"My Aunt Evie lives here, too. Evie Labrecque."

"Evie Labrecque is your aunt? Well, of course she is. I can see a family resemblance now. You're both beautiful."

"Thank you." I'd have to tell Aunt Evie she had an admirer.

"That woman has a fearsome amount of energy. Loves to garden." He looked down at the photos again, shuffling through them until he came to the one of the group at his table. "That poor fellow I was sitting next to died. What a terrible business."

"Actually, I wanted to ask you about that. Did you know Ben well?"

"No, not at all. Never met him before that night."

Well, there went any idea that Neville might be the murderer—not that I would have believed that for a minute.

"From the photo it looks as though you swapped meals with him. Is that right?"

"Yes, he wanted the beef. Said chicken didn't agree with him. I heard him ask his wife to swap but she wouldn't, so then he asked me. It looked very nice," he added in a wistful tone.

"It was," I assured him.

"Still, that red wine sauce probably would have been too rich for me. The old digestive system doesn't work as well as it used to, you know. So I was happy to oblige him. Chicken is much kinder on the tummy. Why do you ask?"

I hesitated. I felt as though giving voice to my suspicions made them real, and I didn't want them to be. How could I look into those smiling blue eyes and tell him someone was trying to kill him?

But how could I not? I would never forgive myself if I kept quiet, trusting that Detective McGovern knew what he was doing, and then something happened to my new friend, Neville. I had to tell him.

Before the pause became too awkward, I screwed up my courage. "I was wondering if someone ... ah ... if someone might have been trying to kill you instead."

He blinked owlishly, his eyes huge behind his glasses. "I beg your pardon? Someone trying to kill *me*?"

"I know it sounds crazy, but when I looked at that photo and saw that you had swapped meals with the man who died, I wondered if the poison had been meant for you instead. Oh, dear, are you all right?"

He had a hand to his throat, and he'd gone very pale. I jumped up and knelt by his chair. His hand was warm, the skin paper-thin in my hand. "I'm sorry, that must be a shock. I shouldn't have come out with it so baldly."

He gave a shaky laugh. "I don't think there's any way to tell someone gently that someone wants to kill them. Was the poison in the meal, then? I thought it must have been in his glass."

"I don't actually know." Somehow, I had to find out. "Detective McGovern wouldn't tell me."

"So you've spoken to the police? Did they agree?"

I frowned. "Detective McGovern wasn't interested in my theory. He says they're close to arresting someone for the murder."

"But that's good, isn't it?" His hand clenched on mine. "That means it wasn't me the murderer was after."

"Only if Detective McGovern is right."

"I see." If possible, he went a little paler. "I wonder if you could get me a glass of water."

"Of course."

I hurried to the kitchen and filled a glass at the sink. He had to hold it with both hands, but his colour looked a little better after he'd had a few sips.

"So if the police are wrong and you are right ..."

"You may be in danger," I said, resuming my seat. "That's why I wanted to talk to you. Can you think of any reason someone might be trying to kill you?"

He shook his head slowly. "Heavens, no. I don't really see anyone except Kim—she's my daughter—and her family. And the residents here, of course. And I can't imagine why any of them would want to kill me. They're a nice bunch. I barely even leave the house these days, except to go to the doctor's. The wedding was a big deal for me. I was very tired afterwards. I wouldn't have made the effort except that it was for Molly."

"Anyone in your past? Enemies from your younger days? People from work?"

That brought a shadow of his usual smile to his face. "If I had any enemies in my youth, they've waited rather a long time, wouldn't you say? All they need to do is hang on for another couple of years and Mother Nature will likely take care of the problem for them. But to answer your question, no. No enemies, and I've been retired for donkey's years. I live a small life these days, Charlie. I don't even drive anymore. I depend on Kim to drive me everywhere."

"I'm sorry," I said, thinking of my own car-less state. "That must be annoying."

"Well, it was time. It happens to us all in the end, doesn't it? Luckily Kim only works part-time, so she can fit in all my trips to the doctor." He gave a little laugh. "There are certainly a lot of them! I lost my licence last year after I had a car accident."

"Oh, dear. Were you all right? What happened?"

"I'm not even sure myself. I was turning into the carpark at Coles, and I just didn't see the car coming towards me. I don't know how I missed it, but I drove straight into him. Made a real mess of his driver's side door. After that they wanted me to go for a driving test to keep my licence, but the accident rattled my confidence so much I decided it would be better just to give it up. I'm just as happy now to be chauffeured around by Kim.

Goodness knows I drove her around enough when she was young."

I laughed. "So it's your turn now?"

"Absolutely. Everyone should live long enough to become a problem to their children, I say. It pays them back for all the sleepless nights they gave us when they were teenagers." He beamed at me. "Not that I don't pay her back in other ways, of course. She's turning fifty next week. I can hardly believe my little girl is fifty, but time moves on for all of us. She's a mother herself now. I've ordered a special bracelet for her from Randall Clifford as a birthday present. She's been so good to me, always driving me around and never a complaint—she's my only child, you know, so it all falls on her. She deserves a treat. She's always loved his designs, but she'd never spend that kind of money on herself. Always thinking of others, that's my Kimmy. I want to make her feel like a queen, at least for a day."

He really was a delight. I hated to break the mood, now that he'd recovered from the shock, but I had to ask. I indicated the group photo that still rested on his skinny knee. "I was just wondering if you know the person sitting next to you at the wedding? His name's Larry, I believe."

Nick's surly friend hulked next to tiny Neville in the photo. If the poison had really been meant for Neville, Larry would have had the best opportunity to add it to his food.

"Oh, yes, of course. He's Kim's husband. He took me to the wedding. Kim was meant to come with me, but at the last minute she had to pull out because Niamh was sick.

That's my granddaughter. A sweet little thing, but she's very clingy, especially when she's not feeling well. You know how kids are."

I didn't, but I nodded sagely anyway. "So Larry took you instead?"

"Yes. It was very kind of him. I'm not so steady on my pins these days. Kim didn't think it was right for him to drop me there and just leave me to manage on my own. I really need help walking any kind of distance. So he came in her place."

"It was a shame for Kim to miss it." I couldn't imagine Larry would have had the same interest in the wedding of his father-in-law's old neighbour as she would have.

"It was." He looked up at me, his eyes bright. "But at least now I have these lovely photos to show her."

CHAPTER 17

RUFUS APPEARED NEXT MORNING WHEN I OPENED THE DOOR TO the inevitable flower delivery. He wandered through the bushes that separated our two driveways and presented himself to Steve for a pat.

"Good boy," Steve said, leaning down to rub those silky ears. "Haven't seen you for a while."

"That's because nobody ever sends me flowers, Steve Orrick." Mrs Johnson's voice was unexpected and I stepped outside. She was standing on her porch, watching Rufus.

"You need to get yourself an admirer like Charlie's," Steve said.

"Or just take his flowers anyway," I suggested. I took the flowers from Steve—white roses today, with a beautiful fragrance—and handed the bouquet across the hedge to her.

"I've still got the last lot you gave me," she protested, but I pushed them at her until she took them.

"Well, I don't want them," I said firmly. "Someone should get some enjoyment out of them."

Steve said goodbye and headed off to make the rest of his rounds. Mrs Johnson breathed in the sweet scent of the roses and sighed. "This takes me back. I used to be quite the gardener, you know. But my knees went years ago and now my hips are getting so stiff I can hardly walk some days." She gazed pensively at Rufus. "I'd move into Sunrise Lodge tomorrow if it wasn't for that dog. The house is just about all I can manage anymore. My poor garden is going to rack and ruin."

"It still looks better than mine," I assured her. I was no gardener and it showed. Weeds were popping up everywhere in the warm weather and some of them were almost as tall as the flowers. "Would you like me to take Rufus for a walk?"

"I don't want to impose on you, dear. I'm sure he'd be just as happy to wander off on his own. You don't need to supervise him, you know."

Mrs Johnson had a lot of faith in her dog, and I did, too, but I had less in people. I was afraid somebody would report him as a stray one day. Rufus could always find his own way home if left to his own devices, but not if someone had locked him up in the pound.

"It's no trouble," I said. "It's such a lovely day I was about to go for a walk anyway."

It was Saturday morning, and I was giving myself the day off.

"Well, if you're sure." She didn't need more persuading than that and went back inside.

I grabbed a hat and my sunnies and stuffed my phone and wallet into my back pockets. A walk on the beach could always end at the surf club café, after all. Since it was Saturday, the beach and café would both be busy, but a takeaway coffee or even an ice cream if I got too hot sounded like a nice way to while away a lazy morning.

Rufus loped over as soon as I called him, his ears pricked with interest. He seemed to enjoy these walks of ours as much as I did, ranging off to check out the smells, then circling back to my side with a happy doggy grin. He liked to make sure I was keeping up with him.

The Nippers were training on the beach near the surf club, dashing in and out of the water, their red and yellow diving caps marking their little heads as they bobbed in the waves and splashed back and forth. The surf club wasn't just a place to go for a meal or a wedding, it had an important function in the life of the local community. Volunteer lifesavers patrolled the beach every weekend and during school holidays, and part of their role was to train up the next generation of swimmers and lifesavers. One day these Nippers would be grown men and women responsible for saving lives, but today they were a bunch of brown-skinned kids shrieking in delight in the waves. Rufus was a bit of a distraction for a few of them, so I steered him away from the water's edge and up towards the café.

As expected, the place was jumping this morning. There wasn't a single table free and there were three people queued at the takeaway window. I joined the line, half keeping an eye on Rufus's activities and half thinking about what I had learned from Neville yesterday. No enemies, as Detective McGovern had said. Maybe I was barking up the wrong tree entirely and the grumpy detective was right. Ben Cassar had been the intended victim all along, and Detective McGovern had the investigation well in hand.

If only I could believe that.

"Charlie!" A high, piping voice shrieked behind me. A small hot body cannoned into my side as I turned.

"Hello, Maisie." This was an unexpected pleasure. Curtis's daughter was a cute little moppet, six years old and full of sunshine and rainbows. She grinned up at me, her dark brown eyes huge in her little pointed face, her curly hair a happy tangle.

"Is this your doggy?" She dropped to her knees and patted Rufus's head carefully. "I love him!"

"His name's Rufus. He belongs to my neighbour; he just comes walking with me sometimes. Where's your dad? Or your mum," I added hurriedly.

Although, I admit, my heart had started thumping at the prospect of seeing her delectable dad again. He often seemed to have her on weekends.

"He's coming," she said, standing up and slipping her hand into mine with the easy confidence that we were friends. Amazing what a shared love of fairy bread could do for a kid. "I did my best running and he couldn't keep up."

I grinned. That was very hard to believe, considering her father was the extremely fit Curtis Kane. I looked around and found him staggering dramatically across the sand toward us, clutching his chest as if he were about to drop dead on the spot.

"See?" Maisie said triumphantly. "I was too fast for him."

"You're a real speed demon," he said to her as he joined us. I noticed that he wasn't breathing hard, even if Maisie didn't. "Hi, Charlie. Join us for a coffee? We owe you one."

"Oh, yes, please!" Maisie jumped up and down on the spot, pipe-cleaner arms flapping excitedly. "Have breakfast with us. They have strawberry shortcake on Saturdays."

"Well, I don't know." There wasn't a seat in the house for love or money. But of course at that very moment a young couple stood up and walked away, and Maisie darted in, claiming the table. "I was just going to get a takeaway coffee. I've already had breakfast."

"Let me get that for you instead and you can help me keep Maisie entertained," Curtis said. "She's taken a real fancy to you. She's been asking me for weeks when we could visit you again."

Rufus plonked himself beside her chair and rested his big head on her lap. She looked up at me, eyes shining with delight, and my heart almost melted.

I'd taken a fancy to her, too. The little lift in my spirits had *nothing* to do with the prospect of spending time with her gorgeous father. Curtis Kane had his daughter's chocolate brown eyes and a sweet smile that made you feel like you were the only person in the room when he turned it on you.

"That's probably more the effect of the fairy bread than me." Maisie and I had discovered a shared love of that sweet treat when she and Curtis had visited me a while back—even though she thought it should be cut into squares, not triangles. *Sacrilege.*

He smiled fondly at his daughter. "It's true she can be bought, but you shouldn't underrate your own charms."

My cheeks heated. Had Curtis spent any time thinking about my charms? "Well, I'd love to catch up with Miss Maisie." And then I hurried to join her, turning my back to her father so he wouldn't see me blush like a schoolgirl. I was twenty-nine years old, for goodness sake, and I certainly wasn't looking for a romance. There was just something about Curtis Kane that made my heart beat a little faster.

The waitress popped out of the café the minute Curtis's muscled posterior hit the chair. "What can I get you, Officer?" She all but batted her eyelids at him. Clearly I wasn't the only woman who appreciated a handsome man when she saw one.

"You don't have to call him Officer today, Penny," Maisie said reprovingly. "He's not on duty."

"Sure. I'll remember that," Penny said with an easy smile at the little girl.

"You can tell because he's not wearing his uniform."

"Uh-huh. Are you having the strawberry shortcake today?"

Maisie looked pensive. "I don't know."

"You lured me here with promises of strawberry short-cake," I reminded her.

She shot a sly glance at her father. "But what if they have something even better? If I don't go and look, I won't know."

"That's true," I said. "You should always consider all the possibilities before making a choice, especially where cake is concerned."

She nodded. "Cake is serious."

"Would you like to go with Penny and look at the selection?" Curtis asked with suitable gravity.

"I think I should."

She slid from her chair and took Penny's hand.

"I'll have the all-you-can-eat breakfast," Curtis told Penny. "Maisie will have a fried egg on toast and whatever she wants from the cake selection. And Charlie's just having a coffee." He quirked an eyebrow at me. "Unless the strawberry shortcake sounds particularly appealing? Would you like to check out the serious cake selection too?"

"I'm good. A latte will be fine, thanks."

Penny nodded. "Come on, Maisie. Let's go get you organised."

When they'd gone, Curtis picked up one of the sugar sachets and began to fiddle with it. It looked tiny in his enormous hands. Curtis Kane was like the supersize me option on the policeman menu. Everything about him was large—even, I suspected from the way he treated his daughter, his heart. "How have you been?"

"Good, thanks. Been busy with the wedding photos this week." How much should I tell him? He would probably know the answer to my question about the poison, but would he be any more likely than Detective McGovern to share? I thought of Neville's beaming smile and screwed up my courage for more rejection. "Actually, I've been doing a bit of thinking. About the murder."

"What kind of thinking?"

For answer, I pulled out my phone and found the photo of table ten on my website. Then I scooted my chair over closer so he could see it. His aftershave smelled amazing. I took a deep breath, trying not to be too obvious about it.

"The kind of thinking that says those two people have the same meal, when the waiters laid them down in an alternating order." I pointed to Gail and Ben's plates. "They both have the beef. And these two people"—I indicated Neville's plate and the half-seen one belonging to his son-in-law, Larry—"both have chicken."

He smelled of fresh forests and sun-warmed days. On top of his ridiculously good looks, it was just unfair. His brown hair was cut almost military-short, which only served to highlight the strong line of his jaw. Eyelashes so long and thick they almost looked fake framed warm brown eyes that shone with intelligence. Mother Nature had been *way* too generous when she was creating him— how was I supposed to concentrate on this very important conversation when I kept wanting to sneak glances at him frowning at the photo? His hand brushed mine as he took the phone and studied the picture more closely.

"So two of them swapped?"

"Yes. Neville said Ben wanted the beef, so he swapped his beef for Ben's chicken."

He sucked in a thoughtful breath. "So Ben might not have been the murderer's target after all."

"Yes!" I was so delighted that he'd seen the issue so quickly I wanted to hug him. Well, that and the fact that he smelled like heaven. It took me a minute to realise that his reply confirmed my suspicions. "So the poison *was* in the meal?"

"I probably shouldn't tell you." He stared at the photo, still frowning. "Let's just say that you seem to be on the right track." Those rich brown eyes caught mine. "And you didn't hear anything from me."

"Got it."

"I need to show this photo to McGovern. I wonder if he's realised the significance of the order of the meals on the table."

"Don't worry, I already told him. He wasn't interested. He seems convinced the killer was after Ben all along. Says they're about to make an arrest. I'm afraid he's going after Troy."

"Hmm." He worried at his lower lip with his teeth.

"But what if he's wrong? What if Neville is still in danger?"

"Who's Neville?" Maisie asked as she climbed back into her seat.

"A friend of mine." Since it didn't seem appropriate to discuss the murder in front of her, I asked her about her cake selection. "Did they have the strawberry shortcake?"

Her face lit up. "Of course. It *is* Saturday. I really wanted it but there was a donut with pink icing and sprinkles and I never had that one before. Daddy says it's always good to try new things, don't you, Dad?"

"Absolutely." He winked at me, which started an unexpected flutter in the pit of my stomach. Although, maybe it shouldn't have been all that unexpected, considering how much I'd just been ogling the guy. "Especially when the new thing involves pink icing and sprinkles."

"Sprinkles make the world go around," I agreed with a smile for Maisie.

We chatted easily until Penny came back with our drinks. The coffee smelled delicious and tasted even better and I sighed in sheer bliss. Sunshine, good company, and coffee—what could be better?

"Nothing beats that first coffee of the day," Curtis said appreciatively as he put his own cup back in the saucer.

"Couldn't agree more," I said, closing my eyes for a moment and tipping my head up to the sun. Speckles of light danced behind my eyelids.

"The view's pretty good, too. Couldn't ask for a nicer start to the day."

I opened my eyes again to find that warm chocolate gaze centred on me and my stomach did that strange little flutter again.

"Daddy, you can't see the view," Maisie pointed out. She and I were facing the beach and the view across the bay; he was sitting with his back to it.

He grinned at her. "I was talking about the two lovely ladies I'm having breakfast with."

She considered me. "Charlie *is* very pretty. But I'm prettier, aren't I?"

"You're *much* prettier," I assured her, hoping my blush wasn't obvious. *Play it cool, Charlie. He's just being sweet to his daughter.*

She patted my hand comfortingly. "Only because you're old. I bet you were just as pretty as me when you were six."

Curtis coughed, trying to disguise a laugh. "I see you're not wearing the neck brace anymore. Are you over the whiplash?"

"Pretty much. Just the occasional twinge now and then."

"And how are things going with the insurance company? Have you got your new car yet?"

"Actually, I had a phone call from them yesterday. They said it will be ready to pick up on Friday. I'll have to ask Aunt Evie to give me a ride down to Newcastle to get it." Breakfast appeared and Curtis cut Maisie's egg on toast into bite-sized pieces. She didn't have to ask and he didn't offer; he just leaned over and did it for her and it warmed my heart. He was such a devoted dad. "Poor Aunt Evie. She's done nothing but drive me around lately. She'll probably throw a party when I finally get the new car."

"Then don't ask her." Curtis attacked his breakfast sausage with enthusiasm, speaking between mouthfuls. "I can take you to Newcastle. Kelly's working on a modelling job in the Hunter Valley and I have to drop Maisie down to her on Friday afternoon after school. It would be no trouble to take you with us."

"Ooh, yes." Maisie's eyes went round with excitement.

"Come with us! Daddy won't play his boring music in the car if you're with us."

He shot her a glance of mock reproval. "It's not boring music, young lady, it's classical."

She pulled a face at him. "Like I said. Boring. They don't even *sing*," she said, turning to me in outrage. "It's just a lot of violins and stuff."

I had to laugh at that. "Are you sure?" I asked him. "I don't want to inconvenience you." I did, however, like the sound of getting to know Curtis a little better. Just as a friend, of course. I could always do with another friend. As Maisie said, it was good to try new things—and I could try a friendship with a man without any romantic intentions.

"Honestly, it's no trouble at all," he said. "We're going through Newcastle anyway, and I'm sure we'd both enjoy your company. Wouldn't we, Maisie Moo?"

She nodded vigorously, since her mouth was full of egg.

"Then that would be marvellous. Thank you." I took another sip of my coffee. They made it just the way I liked it here—not too strong, and not at all bitter. It was rich and creamy and tasted like heaven on my tongue. A feeling of warm contentment stole over me as I listened to Maisie argue with her father about what the best flavour of ice cream was. This was nice. Handsome man, sweet child, divine coffee, and all within a few steps of the ocean. The sound of the waves made a pleasant counterpoint to the rattle of cutlery and the conversations of the other customers around us. I'd made the right decision in leaving Sydney. This place nourished my soul.

Suddenly a new noise intruded. Someone right behind me strummed a guitar and the chatter in the café died away as people looked over curiously. I looked around too and a thrill of horror surged through me.

It was Will.

CHAPTER 18

WHERE HAD HE GOTTEN THAT GUITAR? I HADN'T EVEN KNOWN HE could play. We'd been together for years, and he'd never mentioned any interest in guitar.

He strummed another chord and stepped closer, a big smile on his face. "This one's for you, Charlie."

The next chord had a discordant twang, and his smile slipped a little, then he cleared his throat and launched into the opening bars of one of my favourite love songs. Rufus gave him a doubtful glance, then returned his attention to the far more important task of begging bits of toast from Maisie.

"You know this guy?" Curtis muttered.

I nodded. This was awful. A group of girls at the table next to us was sniggering and everyone was staring. My face was aflame.

"Please stop," I said to Will. His voice was unpleasantly nasal, and his guitar skills were beginner at best. I suspected he may have spent the last two weeks learning just enough to play this song, because he knew it was a favourite of mine. "You're making a scene."

He paused before launching into the chorus. "You said you wanted more romance, so I'm being romantic."

People who said you should be careful what you wished for were right. He tried for a high note and missed so badly that a man walking past winced.

"He's my ex," I said to Curtis. I must have looked like a beetroot. I was so embarrassed that I wanted to sink right into the sand and disappear.

"He's not a very good singer, is he?" Maisie said, in her piping six-year-old's voice, and several of the onlookers laughed.

I was too embarrassed to laugh, but it did make me feel better. Will shot her a dirty look, which rolled off her skinny shoulders unregarded. She was far too interested in the pink and sprinkled donut which had arrived partway through the chorus. Rufus was even more interested.

Will moved closer and went down on one knee in the sand, the guitar propped over his leg.

"Get up," I begged. "That's enough."

No one needed their peaceful Saturday breakfast interrupted by bad singing. But he forged on into the second verse, gathering a crowd of onlookers. I wished he would stand up. Being on one knee made it look horribly like a proposal.

"I'm so sorry about this," I said to Curtis in an undertone. "We broke up and he's not taking it well."

I hated having to explain even that much. I didn't want Will intruding on my new life. The contentment I'd been feeling had been destroyed, and now my stomach was coiled into anxious knots.

Curtis frowned, a steely look entering those warm brown eyes. "Is he stalking you? Do you need me in my official capacity?" He turned a glare on Will that might have given him pause if he'd been looking, but he was still staring at me with single-minded focus.

Honestly, even if the singing had been divine and his advances welcome, I still would have been embarrassed. I was all for public displays of affection, but there were limits. I didn't want my love life to be a show that was put on for the entertainment of strangers. The crowd was getting bigger and I heard one woman ask her friend, "Do you think she'll say yes?" I wanted to run, but I couldn't just abandon Curtis and Maisie.

"I can handle it," I said. "It's fine."

It was *so* not fine, but I wouldn't get anyone else involved. I was a big girl.

"It's not fine," Curtis said, his gaze taking in my flushed cheeks and miserable expression. "This is harassment."

He put his knife and fork down and I laid a hand on his arm. "Please don't do anything. It will only make it worse."

"He's upsetting you. I'm not going to sit here and let him get away with that. People have to learn to take no for an answer." He pushed his chair back and stood up, all imposing six foot four of him. I could almost feel the attention of the crowd shift to him, anticipating a clash. I felt sick. "Mate, my daughter's right. You're not a good singer and you're upsetting the lady. I suggest you go have a nice day somewhere else."

Will stood up, too. His head only came to Curtis's shoulder, and he looked like a kid getting into trouble with his dad. "And who are you?" He'd stopped singing, at least, but this wasn't much better. There was aggression in every line of his body as he squared up to Curtis. "Who is he?" he snapped at me over his shoulder.

"He's my daddy," Maisie said firmly, "and he's a policeman and he'll arrest you if you don't do what he says."

That deflated him. He glared at Maisie, but his stance became more defensive, the guitar between his body and Curtis's like a shield. Curtis still stood in the same loose, relaxed pose as before, but his sheer physicality was enough of a threat. He looked like a man who was used to action, not sitting behind a desk.

"I'm not doing anything wrong," Will said. "There's no law against serenading your fiancée."

Curtis glanced at me in surprise.

"*Ex*-fiancée," I said quickly.

"You're creating a public nuisance," Curtis said calmly.

"Arrest him for crimes against music, Kane," one of the onlookers suggested to general laughter.

Someone else clapped Will on the shoulder. "Better luck next time, mate. Try a bunch of flowers. The girls like those."

Will stormed off, his mouth a tight, angry line, and I sagged with relief. Now that the show was over, the crowd dispersed quickly, though not without a few comments that had my face flaming again.

I glanced across at Maisie, who had demolished the pink donut already, with willing assistance from Rufus. She'd quickly lost interest in Will and his bad singing, but I was proud of her contribution. "You're my hero, Maisie. I'm going to buy you a *whole* strawberry shortcake."

CHAPTER 19

I MET UP WITH PRIYA AND HEIDI THAT NIGHT FOR DRINKS AT THE Metropole. Heidi had suggested the surf club, but a man had been murdered there the previous Saturday night. I had no desire to go back so soon. I hadn't been too keen on the Metropole either at first, since Will was staying there, but in the end I decided that I wasn't going to let Will dictate where I could and couldn't go.

The Metropole occupied a commanding position on the southern headland of Sunrise Bay, with a view across the water that took in the whole town as well as the sweep of the crescent-shaped beach. It was an older hotel that had been done up long enough ago that it was in need of renovations again, but it was still grand. I'd been here for drinks with Priya before, but I always enjoyed walking into its art deco interior. I particularly liked the sweeping staircase that curved up from the foyer to the first floor. One day I'd photograph a bride on those stairs—it would look spectacular.

The bar was to the left of the foyer. The double doors with their stained-glass panels stood open, and I walked through and found Heidi and Priya already ensconced at one of the tables by the tall floor-to-ceiling windows.

Priya waved me over with a bright smile. "What's this I hear about some guy serenading you at the café this morning?"

I sank into a spare seat with a groan. "You heard about that?"

"Honey, half of Sunny Bay has heard about it by now. Your love life is the most exciting thing that's happened all week."

"More exciting than murder?" I asked.

She waved a hand dismissively. "Technically, that happened last week."

They already had a bottle of bubbly open in a silver bucket on the table and Heidi poured some into a third glass, then pushed it toward me with a sympathetic smile. "I assume it was your ex?"

I downed half the glass in one go. "Who else?"

"Tell us everything," Priya said impatiently. "Come on, come on, I want the goss."

So I told them the whole thing. They both laughed when I got to Maisie's evaluation of Will's musical talents and how badly he'd reacted to that. When I was finished, Heidi eyed me speculatively. "Sounds like Curtis might be interested in you."

"No, I don't think so. He's just a decent guy, trying to help out." I didn't tell them that he had offered to drive me to Newcastle next Friday. I didn't need any more speculation about my love life, even from my friends.

The talk turned to more general things and soon the bottle of champagne was gone. Priya, of course, ordered another.

"Is it true that journalists can drink lesser beings under the table?" I asked her. "Just wondering if I'm going to need someone to carry me out of here."

"Nonsense," she said firmly as she topped up my glass. "You must be out of practice if you're so worried, and there's only one way to fix that."

"Are you okay?" Heidi asked. "You seem a little quiet tonight. Did Will upset you that much?"

I shrugged. "It's not Will. I've just been thinking a lot about the murder. I'm worried the killer will strike again."

"Again?" Heidi's eyes widened. "But surely now Ben is dead..." She trailed off into silence.

I got out my phone and showed them the photograph and explained my theory. "I'm worried about Neville."

Priya's eyes sparked with interest at the whiff of a story. "Interesting theory." She studied the photo intently, as if it could speak to her. "So who had the opportunity to poison the meal?"

I sighed. "Plenty of people, I guess. Cooks, waiters, some random person passing by, or someone already close at the table. It could almost have been anyone at all out of more than a hundred people who were there that night."

"*I* was there," Priya said.

"So it could have been you," I said. "Anything you'd like to tell us?"

She laughed. "Didn't you suspect me of Peggy's murder at one stage?"

"Charlie!" Heidi gasped.

"Not seriously," I protested.

Priya shook her head in mock outrage. "Such a disturbing lack of trust."

"Surely we can narrow it down a little from a hundred people," Heidi said.

"Well, yes. I doubt it was the chefs, or even the waiters. The poison would have had to have been added to the meal either just before or just after the plate was placed on the table. Before that, the killer couldn't have been sure who would get which one."

Priya rubbed her hands together. "See, that's better! Now we have a much smaller pool of possible killers."

"It could have been Ben's wife," Heidi said, leaning over to inspect the photo again.

"Sure—if Ben was the target," Priya said. "But if Charlie is right, and Neville Botham was meant to die instead, I think we can rule Gail out. What possible reason would she have to kill him?"

We all stared at Neville's smiling face beaming out of the phone at us. What reason could anyone have for killing that sweet old man?

"That's the trouble," I said. "We have plenty of suspects for Ben. I can see why McGovern isn't interested in my theory. He's got a jealous wife, a jilted lover, a disgruntled employee, *and* an angry client. So many options. Troy looks the worst, and I'm sure that's who he's focused on. But Ella and Gail don't look squeaky clean either. And don't tell Andrea—Nick Kettlewell has just as good a motive and opportunity as Troy. But none of them work if the intended victim was Neville."

"So that probably means that it was meant to be Ben and you don't need to worry about Neville," Heidi said encouragingly.

"Or it means Neville's a sitting duck if she's right," Priya pointed out.

I sighed. "Thanks, Priya, that's very reassuring."

"Did you see anyone moving around the table in the right timeframe?" Heidi asked me.

"I wasn't really paying attention," I admitted. "I was so focused on doing a good job. A couple of people bumped me walking past but I barely glanced at them. I know there were people walking around but I couldn't tell you who. Well, except Nick. He was definitely out of his seat at the right time."

"One of the other people at the table could have done it while they were getting in place for the photo," Heidi said.

"True," Priya said. "Who is this grumpy-looking guy next to Neville? Seems like he would have had the best opportunity."

"That's his son-in-law, Larry."

"Oh, is that Kim Brandt's husband?" Heidi asked.

"Um ... could be. I know Neville has a daughter called Kim. Do you know her?"

"She knows everybody," Priya said. "She's worse than me."

"I don't know everybody!" Heidi protested. "There are

almost ten thousand people in this town—how could I know them all? But I do know a lot of the ones with kids. And I don't *know her* know her. She's been into the shop a few times, that's all. Seems like a nice woman."

I shrugged. "She probably is. And Larry is probably a nice guy, too. And here we are, busy smearing his good character under the influence of all this champagne. I mean, why would he want to kill his own father-in-law?"

Heidi burst out laughing. "Clearly you've never been married. In-laws can be the bane of your existence."

I stared at her in surprise over the top of my champagne flute. It wasn't like Heidi to have a bad word for anyone. "You don't get on with your in-laws?"

"Oh, no, my in-laws are wonderful!" Phew! My faith in the universe was restored. "But from what my friends say, I realise that not everyone is as lucky as me."

Priya rested her elbows on the table and propped her chin in her hands. "Could be money. That's always a good motive. Maybe the old guy is loaded and Larry's impatient to get his hands on the inheritance."

"That could work," I said. People had been known to do some terrible things for money. "But where would he get his hands on the cyanide?" Unless he'd been behind the break-in at Nick's parents' house and had stolen Nick's developing gear—but I didn't know whether Nick had actually had cyanide or not. And would he have left it lying around his parents' basement if he had? "Where would anyone get it, for that matter? I imagine there must be all sorts of regulations governing the sale of something so dangerous."

Priya pulled out her phone with a gleam in her eye. "Leave this to me. I live for this kind of thing."

She pulled up Google and started typing away, thumbs flying. I sat back and admired the view out the windows while I waited for the results of her research. It was dark outside, of course, so the water was largely invisible, but the lights of the town below us glinted prettily in the darkness.

"I bet you could buy it on the dark web if you knew where to look," Heidi said.

I eyed her doubtfully. "Would a regular person know how to access the dark web?"

"Regular people don't go around murdering other people," she said. I had to admit she had a point.

"You don't need the dark web," Priya said after a bit of clicking around and scanning websites. "Sale and purchase of cyanide is regulated in Australia, but some laboratories would have it, for sure. Says here cyanide is also used in agriculture, photography, and gold mining, to name just a few. Even goldsmithing. And it's in some jewellery-cleaning solutions. Apparently some people have tried to kill themselves by drinking that."

"Oh, that's awful," Heidi said, ever sympathetic.

"So we're looking for a farmer, or a photographer," Priya said, then turned a mock-stern look on me. "You're a photographer. Where were you on the night of the fifth of November?"

"Very funny. I don't develop my own photos."

Although Nick had, at one stage. He could even be lying about the break-in and the theft of his darkroom gear to throw me off the scent. Maybe he was the murderer—although if it was him, Neville was safe. Nick would have been after Ben, for sure.

"Or it could be a jeweller," Heidi said. "They would all have jewellery-cleaning solutions. What's a goldsmith? Is that the same as a jeweller?"

Priya held up one finger then went back to her research. A moment later she had the answer. "A goldsmith is the person who makes the jewellery. A jeweller is the person who buys it and resells to the public." She looked up. "There's a goldsmith in Waterloo Bay, isn't there? Randall something."

"Randall Clifford," Heidi said. "He's the guy who made Molly and Marco's rings."

"Her engagement ring was out of this world," I said.

"Probably out of this world price-wise, too," Heidi said. "I was too scared to even go into his shop when we were looking at rings. Everything is so expensive."

"Maybe I should pay him a visit," I said, "and see if he's misplaced any cyanide recently."

CHAPTER 20

I GOT MY CHANCE ON MONDAY MORNING. AUNT EVIE HAD AN appointment with her eye specialist in Waterloo Bay, and she wanted me to come along to drive her home.

"He always puts those hideous drops in my eyes," she said. "I can't see a thing afterwards. Normally I would just call a taxi, but now that you're here you can come along. It will do you good to get behind the wheel again."

I did my best not to feel as though this was a scam to force me to drive again. Not that I minded helping her out, of course, but that triumphant gleam in her eye made me suspicious.

"I'll be picking up my car on Friday," I pointed out. "So I'll be getting behind the wheel pretty soon anyway."

"You should practise first," she said firmly. "It can be nerve-wracking enough to get used to driving a new car without adding anything else into the mix. I'll come over to your place and you can drive us both there."

So that was what we did. People had a way of falling in

with Aunt Evie's plans, since she always acted as if there was no other option. I was a little jumpy on the drive to Waterloo Bay. It wasn't far—only ten minutes—but that was plenty of time to shy away from half a dozen cars that seemed too close, and to spend way too long checking my rear vision mirror for signs of vehicles coming up behind me.

Still, it was a relief to have my first time driving again behind me, and I felt good when I stepped out of the car in Nelson Street. Not that I would ever admit as much to Aunt Evie.

"We're a little early," she said. "Shall we go for a walk?"

"Sure."

We set off down the street, stopping occasionally to check out a window display.

"How are you going with your investigation?" she asked. "Have you cleared Troy yet?"

I snorted. "While I love your faith in me, I have to point out that it's only been a week. But I don't think Troy should even be a suspect anymore."

"Because of the swapped meals?"

"That's right. Troy's only a suspect if the victim was supposed to be Ben. I don't know who to look at for Neville."

She stopped to admire a dress in a soft pink that would look lovely on her. "Who inherits if he dies?"

"Presumably, his daughter Kim. She's an only child."

"There you are, then."

"You said the same thing about Peggy's daughter!" I

objected. "Do you always suspect people's children? Is there something you want to tell me about your relationship with Brenda?"

Brenda was Aunt Evie's daughter, who currently lived in Perth, on the other side of the country, so we didn't see much of her. She was thirteen years older than me and had children in high school and a thriving online coaching business.

She tossed her head and started walking again. "Don't be silly, dear. It's just Oxford's Law, isn't it?"

"What's Oxford's Law?"

"That the most obvious answer is usually the correct one."

I laughed. "Aunt Evie, that's Occam's Razor."

"Is it? Well, no need to quibble about the details. The point still stands."

"Occam's Razor didn't work last time."

She shrugged. "There are exceptions to every rule. It doesn't mean the rule is wrong."

I rolled my eyes. There was no arguing with her once she'd set her mind on something. "I wouldn't mind visiting Randall Clifford's. Do you know where it is?"

She gestured across the street at the cinema. "Just around the corner from the cinema. Jo London works there."

"Who's Jo London?" I asked as we crossed the road.

"One of Brenda's friends."

Randall Clifford's shop had very few pieces in the window, which signalled at once that it was expensive and exclusive. None of them had prices on them, either, which was another sign. It was the classic *if you have to ask, you can't afford it* scenario. A bell chimed discreetly as we entered the air-conditioned quiet, and a familiar face looked up from where she was cleaning a glass counter.

It was Jo from the wedding—the one who'd cried during the ceremony, who'd been sitting next to Andrea. She looked better today, and smiled warmly at Aunt Evie.

"Hi, Evie. Nice to see you. How's Brenda?"

"She's as busy as ever. You know Brenda. How have you been, dear?"

"Oh, you know. Up and down."

Aunt Evie smiled sympathetically. "It's good to see you back at work."

Jo's smile became tremulous and I remembered she'd lost her husband. Recently? I thought Andrea had said last year, but I couldn't recall.

"It's better to keep busy," she said, then drew herself up and offered a professional smile. "Now, is there something I can help you with?"

Clearly she didn't want to discuss her personal situation anymore, and who could blame her? I remembered what it had been like after Mum died. For months I'd run into people who hadn't seen me for a while, and they'd ask how I was in such hushed tones they may as well have screamed, "How are you coping with the loss of your mother?"

It shouldn't have made a difference—it wasn't as though I only thought about Mum if someone mentioned her. I thought about her all the time. I was sad all the time. But somehow the way people looked at me with such sorrow and asked, "how are you *feeling*?" with such peculiar emphasis made me want to scream.

"We're just browsing today," Aunt Evie said. "My niece wanted to have a look. Have you met Charlie?"

"Not officially," I said, "but I saw you at the wedding."

She blanched. "What a dreadful business. I feel so sorry for that poor man's wife."

"It's terrible," Aunt Evie agreed.

I wandered away and left them chatting. There were some beautiful pieces on display. One necklace in a case on its own looked fit for an Aztec queen. It was probably worth a king's ransom.

I saw a very pretty ring that was similar to Molly's engagement ring, with a matching bracelet that made me wish I'd won the lottery recently. I loved the way the different colours of gold were woven together. Randall Clifford might know how to charge, but he also knew his goldsmithing.

The man himself appeared while I was wandering his shop. At least, I assumed it was him. Nobody else would be appearing from what was clearly a workshop area. I caught a glimpse of high benches scattered with tools before he closed the door behind him and stepped into the store.

He was an older man, probably close to retirement age. His silver hair was brushed back in distinguished waves, and his thick fingers were weighed down by several heavy gold rings. He smiled as he approached me.

"Can I interest you in something?"

"I was just admiring this one," I said. "I saw the rings

you made for Molly Lombardi. They were absolutely beautiful."

"Thank you." He smiled, but I had the sense that he considered the praise only what was due to him. "And now you're looking for an engagement ring yourself?"

I shuddered. "Not at all."

I'd given Will's ring back to him. Pulled it off my finger and thrown it in his face, actually, the minute I'd found him in bed with Amy. It had bounced off his bare chest and rolled under the bed. As far as I was concerned, it could stay there forever, but no doubt the accountant in Will hadn't been able to leave such a valuable asset to go to waste.

Not that it had cost anything like what Randall Clifford probably charged for his wares. We'd bought it from a chain store, not an actual goldsmith.

"Your work must be very interesting," I said, hoping to get him talking. "Where do you get your inspiration from? That one looks rather Aztec, or Mayan."

He smiled, and this time it was more genuine. "You've hit the nail right on the head. I do get a lot of my inspiration from other cultures. But inspiration can be found anywhere, if you only look at things with the right eyes. A leaf, a bird, architecture, the pattern on a piece of cloth. Anything."

I gestured again at the Aztec-inspired necklace. "So would you make something like that on commission?"

"That one is on spec, but I don't truly imagine it will ever sell. It's more to display my design chops." He smiled fondly at the beautiful gold necklace. "I think I'd miss it if anyone actually bought it. It's been with me so long."

"Is most of your work on commission, then?"

"Yes. Probably ninety per cent, I'd say. I hardly ever get time these days just to play around. The perils of success. Still, commissions can be quite a ride themselves. I had a lady ask me once to make her a ring that contained her boyfriend's blood in a glass vial where the stone would normally be."

"How odd."

"I presume she thought it was romantic."

I hoped Will never heard of such a thing. In his current mood, who knew what he might come up with?

"I suppose you must use a lot of chemicals in your work." Finally, I'd worked my way around to the question I really wanted to ask. "Do you have anything super dangerous back there in the workshop?"

He frowned. "You're the second person who's asked me that lately. It's this terrible business with that poor chap at the wedding. The police have been around asking about cyanide."

"Do you use cyanide in your work?"

"Yes, I use it in the stripping process to make the gold brighter. But of course I don't leave it around for anyone to find. It's a dangerous chemical and there are very strict protocols for dealing with it. It's always locked up tighter than Fort Knox."

"I imagine you would only need a tiny amount to kill a person. Would you notice if only a little was missing?"

He frowned and a stern note crept into his voice. "I can

assure you, as I assured the police, that every precaution is taken. It is kept under lock and key and no one but me has access to it." He patted his pocket and I heard the jingle of keys. "You must excuse me now, but please enjoy your time browsing the shop."

He exchanged a few words with Jo and Aunt Evie, then went out into the street. I watched him stride away, feeling as though I'd just been reprimanded by the head-master. He hadn't seemed at all impressed by the implication that he was careless with the dangerous chemicals of his trade.

Oh, well. I gave a mental shrug. I couldn't be responsible for the fragile egos of every man I came across.

Aunt Evie looked at her watch. "We'd better head off, too, Charlie. My appointment's in five minutes. They nearly always run late, but you know how it is—the first time *I* was late, Dr Eugene would be standing there tapping his foot waiting for me."

"No problem." We said goodbye to Jo and set off for Aunt Evie's appointment.

"Poor Jo," she said pensively as we walked. "She's doing remarkably well, really. But it must be so hard."

"Losing her husband, you mean? You know what that's like."

She sighed. "Yes, but my Andy died in his sixties. At least we had a life together. And we created a family—I had the children around me for support. Jo and Xavier had only been married two years. And she's so young! They had their whole lives before them and then, bam—one car accident and it's all snatched away." She shook her head sadly. "I felt so sorry for her, I invited her to join us for our next book club meeting. It would do her good to get out and about again. She seems so isolated. I hope the other ladies won't mind."

"I'm sure they won't. They're a very welcoming bunch."

Her face brightened as we arrived at the eye specialist. "The more the merrier, right?"

CHAPTER 21

ON TUESDAY AFTERNOON, I WAS AT A LOOSE END. IT WAS A RARE rainy day in Sunrise Bay, and even Rufus's most doleful looks couldn't persuade me to take him out for a walk. I had no more photography work—the wedding photos were all up in the online gallery and Molly hadn't placed an order yet, so there was nothing to do there for the moment. I would have been tempted to curl up with a book, except that I was three-quarters of the way through *Sense and Sensibility* and Marianne was becoming seriously annoying. Moping around, taking long walks in the rain— honestly, Willoughby wasn't worth all the drama.

So when the rain finally cleared, I grabbed an umbrella to be on the safe side and headed out. *That's the way it's done, Marianne. No need to try killing yourself with the weather.* Neville was weighing on my mind and I just couldn't sit still any longer.

A few minutes later, I was knocking on the door of a small brick house across the road from the school. A petite blond woman with the dark shadows of the perpetually tired under her eyes opened the door.

"Can I help you?" she asked.

"Hi. My name's Charlie Carter. Could I talk to you for a moment about your dad?"

A worried look entered her eyes. "Are you from the Lodge? Is he all right?"

"He's fine and no, I'm not from the Lodge. I'm just a friend. I'm new in the area but I met Neville at Molly and Marco's wedding. Do you mind if I come in?" I was uncomfortable enough about being here—not because I suspected her, whatever Aunt Evie said, but because I didn't know how she'd take my news. I didn't want to blurt out my suspicions on the doorstep. The poor woman already looked as though a stiff breeze could blow her away. She might need to be sitting down for this.

She held the door wider. "Of course."

She led the way through a small lounge/dining room where two girls of primary school age lay on the floor watching TV. The carpet was scattered with toys and after-school snacks. She stepped over and around them automatically, as if from long practice. In the kitchen she moved a pile of folded washing and offered me a chair, shoving a pile of papers down to one end of the small kitchen table to clear a space.

"Sorry about the mess," she said as she sat down. "I was at work all weekend and Larry never minds what the girls get up to. The place looks like a bomb has hit it."

"Mine is worse," I assured her, "and I don't even have any kids."

She smiled at that and seemed to relax a little. "How did you know where to find me?"

"I was talking to Neville and he told me your name. He talks about you a lot, you know. It was easy enough to find your address in the White Pages."

"So what's this about?"

Now came the tricky part. There really was no easy way to say this kind of thing. "Have you spoken to your dad in the last couple of days?"

"No, not since Saturday morning. Work, you know. I'm due to take him to his heart specialist tomorrow, though, so I'll see him then."

"I went to see him last Friday because I was worried about him." I took out my phone and brought up the photo of table ten to show her.

She smiled. "That's a lovely photo of Dad." The smile faded as she took in the rest of the photo. "That must be the poor man who died next to him, right?" She looked at me for confirmation. "Larry said he was sitting next to Dad."

"Yes, he was. I was the photographer at the wedding, and I was looking at this photo the other day and I noticed that your dad and Ben Cassar, the dead man, had swapped meals." I waited to see if she would draw the obvious conclusion, as Curtis had done, but she continued to watch me expectantly. "It occurred to me that the murderer may have intended to kill your father, not Mr Cassar, and it was only the fact that they swapped meals that meant your dad survived."

Her hands flew to her mouth and her eyes widened.

"You think someone is trying to kill Dad?" She shook her head. "That can't be right. The police would have said something."

Her stare had turned almost fierce. I was guessing I had stirred her protective instincts.

"I have to tell you," I said, "I've already talked to the detective in charge of the case about this."

"And what did he say?"

I shifted uneasily under the weight of her stare. "He didn't want to listen. And I sincerely hope he's right and that this has nothing to do with your dad. But I'm worried. If the police are wrong your dad might still be in danger."

She folded her arms, tucking her hands tightly into her armpits, almost hugging herself, and took three deep breaths. It seemed to calm her. "I can't imagine why anyone would want to hurt Dad. He's one of nature's gentlemen. Wouldn't hurt a fly. How could anyone want to kill him?"

"I was hoping you might be able to shed some light on that." That was the real reason for my visit. "Does he have any enemies?"

"Enemies?" she echoed dazedly. I'd really thrown her for a loop. "I can't think ..." She shook her head. "No. No, of course he doesn't."

A car pulled up outside. The throb of the engine was shut off, soon followed by the slam of a car door. Kim's eyes flicked toward the front door, then back to me.

The sound of the key in the lock heralded the arrival of Larry. I recognised him from the wedding, though today he wore shorts and work boots and a T-shirt emblazoned with the logo of one of the lawnmowing franchises. A whiff of sweat and cut grass swept into the house with him.

"Turn that racket down," he snarled at the kids before he saw me.

The noise from the TV abruptly halved as he stomped into the kitchen, where he regarded me with a suspicious frown. "Who's this?" he asked his wife.

Clearly he didn't recognise me from the wedding. "I'm Charlie Carter," I said, forcing a smile though he loomed in the small room in a very unwelcoming manner. "I met you at Molly and Marco's wedding. I was the photographer."

"You trying to sell us photos? Because we're not buying." He stomped over to the sink where he dumped an empty water bottle on the bench.

"Charlie just dropped in to talk about Dad," Kim said hurriedly.

"What about him?"

"Apparently he swapped meals at the wedding with the man who died. Charlie was wondering if someone might have been trying to kill Dad instead."

He snorted as if he couldn't imagine anything more ridiculous. At least that was better than a guilty start.

"Kill old Neville?" He leaned back against the bench, his arms folded across his spreading stomach. "What on earth for?"

"I'm sure it's nothing," Kim said, rushing to fill the silence. "Of course no one would want to kill Dad."

I hesitated. In the face of Larry's obvious hostility, it

might be better to do this at a later time when I could get Kim to herself. But I wasn't sure how receptive she would be to a further meeting, and I really wanted to know. I took a deep breath. Might as well go the whole hog now I was here. Aunt Evie would be proud. "I was wondering if you knew who benefits from Neville's will?"

Larry uncrossed his arms and took a step forward. "Who benefits ...! Are you accusing *us* of trying to kill him?"

"Of course not," I said hurriedly. I hoped the kids weren't listening to this.

"I'm sure it's nothing like that, sweetie," Kim said, glancing in alarm between me and her husband. "She just wants to know if there's anyone *besides* us. Don't you, Charlie?"

"That's right," I said.

"It's none of your business," he growled, fixing me with that surly look I knew so well from the wedding.

I stood up. It was quite clear I couldn't get any further here. "Just trying to help. I would hate it if anything happened to Neville and I hadn't said anything."

Kim jumped up too. "Sweetie, why don't you grab yourself a beer and relax. You've had a long day."

If she'd been a sheepdog she couldn't have herded me any better towards the front door. The two girls glanced over as Kim opened it, but quickly lost interest as we stepped outside. The lure of their cartoon was too strong.

Kim pulled the door half closed behind her. "I'm sorry about that. Larry's got a bit of a short fuse. He works so hard, you see. My job doesn't bring in much so it's all on him."

"It's fine." I got the feeling she was well practised in placating her husband and maybe even in apologising for him afterwards. "I'm sorry to cause trouble. I'm just really worried about Neville."

"I'm sure it's nothing. There isn't anybody else in the will. I'm an only child, and Dad's left everything to me." She forced a smile. "And I'm hardly likely to murder him, am I?"

"Kim!" Larry roared from somewhere in the depths of the house.

"I'd better go," she said apologetically, then nipped inside and shut the door in my face.

I walked back home, swinging my umbrella, my mood thoughtful. I didn't believe for a moment that Kim would hurt one hair on her father's head. But I couldn't say the same for Larry, whose hostile presence had made me distinctly uncomfortable. His wife was the sole beneficiary. Perhaps he was tired of waiting for her inheritance and had decided to take matters into his own hands.

I sighed. I wasn't used to thinking the worst of people, but recent events were making me paranoid. Larry knew Nick. Had gone to school with him. In fact, Nick had said they'd been in nearly every class together. So Larry must have been well aware that Nick did photography and had his own amateur darkroom. Potentially, he could have gotten cyanide from Nick at some stage.

Maybe he'd even had his own darkroom at some point —he must have been in that same Photography class. Or he could have stolen cyanide from Nick's parents' house during the break-in last year. I wouldn't put it past Larry Brandt to make a bit of extra cash by emptying out the odd house when the owners were away on holidays, particularly if money was as tight as Kim seemed to suggest. He looked like the kind of guy who could be knocking over houses and selling TVs down at the pub.

So far Larry was my prime suspect—and my only one.

CHAPTER 22

THURSDAY NIGHT WAS OUR BOOK CLUB MEETING, WHICH HAD been moved from Tuesday because of another function at the library.

"I'm surprised you didn't suggest a change of venue instead of changing nights," I said to Priya as I settled into a seat beside her.

Andrea had set up a ring of chairs in the children's book section, next to the big windows that looked out over the playground. Colourful displays brightened the walls and a range of beautiful picture books rested invitingly on their stands for the children to dive into. Usually there were a bunch of large floor pillows set out in this space, too, to encourage reading and lounging, but Andrea had stacked them in the corner to make room for our circle.

"You know me so well already." Priya grinned. "I did suggest the Metropole, but Andrea pooh-poohed it."

"I knew that any pretence at a sensible discussion of

the book would drown in champagne and mojitos," Andrea said, overhearing us.

Secretly I wondered if Andrea had ever been a school-teacher. She just had that commanding presence and the knack of organising people. But probably librarians had that, too.

"All right, everyone." She clapped her hands for attention. "It's about time we got started. Sorry to change the night on you—I know that Sarah couldn't make it this time, but I'm happy to see the rest of you."

"Oh, here's Jo," Aunt Evie said, smiling brightly as a new arrival appeared from behind the shelves. "Come in, Jo, and grab a seat." She patted the chair next to her invitingly. "Do you know everyone? Let me introduce you."

A chorus of greetings rose from the circle as Jo sat down. She wore jeans and a T-shirt tonight, which was the most casual I'd ever seen her, but she still had that kind of shadowed look to her eyes that meant she never really looked relaxed.

"I hope you don't mind me joining you all," she said. "I haven't read *Sense and Sensibility* in a few years, but I saw the Emma Thompson movie. I think I remember everything."

Aunt Evie patted her knee. "That's fine, dear."

"There'll be a test at the end," Andrea said, straight-faced.

Jo shot her a startled glance. "Really?"

"She's pulling your leg," Aunt Evie said, giving Andrea a reproving look which the librarian shrugged off like water off a duck's back. "Don't be such a tease, Andrea."

"I'm only kidding."

Jo's face relaxed into a tentative smile, and we launched into our discussion of the book.

"It was another hard one to read," Heidi said. "Those poor women. Their fates were so dependent on marrying well."

"It seems really hard to relate to that kind of thing now," Emily said. She was a pretty Chinese girl who seemed very friendly, but I hadn't caught up with her except at our book club meetings so far. But we seemed to be on the same wavelength here, so I should probably get to know her better. "I can't imagine being that dependent on a man. Why does Austen always write about the same things?"

"What else is she going to write about?" Andrea asked. "It's all she knows. Have you noticed she never even writes a scene where men are on their own? It's because she doesn't know how men talk when the women aren't present and she wants to be as true to life as possible."

"I know they're romances but I find them depressing," Priya said. "Those poor women had such little lives."

"Let's read something completely different next time," I said. "Can't we read a fantasy or some science fiction?"

Aunt Evie looked horrified. "We only read books by dead authors."

"I'm sure there are plenty of dead science fiction authors. The genre has been around for a while, you know."

"Longer than you think," Andrea agreed. "Ever since Mary Shelley wrote *Frankenstein*."

"Let's read that!" I was with Priya—it was time to venture out of Jane Austen's drawing rooms and into the wider world.

"Oh, but I wanted to read *Middlemarch* again for our next book. I'd love to hear everyone's thoughts on it," Aunt Evie said.

"Maybe the one after that, then?"

It took some doing to convince Aunt Evie, but eventually everyone agreed to put *Frankenstein* on the schedule after *Middlemarch*, and Andrea gently steered the conversation back to *Sense and Sensibility*.

"It's certainly dated as far as marriage goes," Heidi said. "And thank goodness things have changed! But it still has some interesting points to make about different personalities and how they deal with the trials and tribulations of romance."

That led into a lively discussion of the personalities of the two sisters. Opinions were fairly evenly split between Team Elinor and Team Marianne. But eventually, as I had feared, attention turned to me, and Marianne and Elinor's troubles were left behind for more contemporary issues.

"I hear you've got some man troubles yourself, Charlie," Andrea said.

She was smiling, but there was a gleam of interest in her eye that told me she wouldn't let up until she had all the details. Fortunately, Priya and Heidi already knew all about Will's abortive serenade, so I could let them do most of the talking.

"Sunrise Bay has certainly been pretty lively lately,"

Andrea said when she was satisfied. "We've never had a troubadour here before."

"Hopefully, you never will again, either," I said.

"*Troubadour* seems a little generous," Priya said. "I heard he sounded like a cat being tortured."

"I don't think we want any more excitement of the murderous kind either," Aunt Evie said. "That poor man at the wedding. I can't believe someone right here in Sunny Bay is running around poisoning people."

"It's awful," Jo agreed. Were those tears in her eyes? "He shouldn't have died."

"I hope the police find whoever did it quickly," Andrea said.

"It might take them a while to sort through all the suspects," Emily said. "Apparently he had quite a few enemies."

Heidi nodded. "Just as well Sarah isn't here tonight. Troy's one of them."

Emily looked startled. "Troy?"

Heidi filled her in on Troy's dealings with the dead man and how Ben had stiffed Troy and Sarah out of their money and left them with a half-built house.

Andrea nodded sagely. "And they're not the only ones, either. There are probably a lot of people in Sunrise Bay at the moment who are happy that Ben Cassar is dead."

She was going out with one of them, so she should know. Aunt Evie went to put on the kettle in the librarians' break room and Heidi brought out a cake. We all drifted around for a while, making cups of tea and chatting.

Emily had to leave early because she still had a ton of

work to get through before the next day. Jo made her excuses soon after and disappeared.

"Do you think Jo enjoyed herself?" Aunt Evie asked, nibbling on a slice of apple tea cake.

"I think so," Heidi said. I was standing with the two of them in front of the windows, where a huge crepe paper tree sprawled over the glass, with monkeys hanging from its branches and an assortment of other jungle animals gathered around its trunk. "She was very quiet, though, so it's hard to tell."

"She seemed upset when we were talking about Ben's death," I said.

"It's probably a little too close to home for her," Heidi said, "if she lost her own husband so suddenly." Aunt Evie had warned everyone before Jo arrived. "It will be bringing it all back to her."

Aunt Evie nodded. "She'd be putting herself in Gail's shoes right now. She knows how it feels. You can see how it would affect the poor girl."

"I know I'd be a basket case if Dave died," Heidi said. "I can't imagine going on without him."

"How *did* Jo's husband die?" I asked. "You said it was in a car accident."

Aunt Evie took a sip of tea, as if to fortify herself. "It was simply awful. A terrible, terrible tragedy. It wasn't actually the car accident that killed him. He walked away from that but his arm was broken in three places. They had to do an operation to put some screws in to hold the bone together while it healed. And then the poor man died on the operating table."

Wow. That really *was* awful. "Why? What happened?"

"He had a heart attack. Apparently he had an undiagnosed heart condition."

"That can happen," Heidi said. "I had a friend whose husband was playing a game of tennis one day. He was a really fit guy, played a lot of sport. He looked so healthy, you know? And he was only in his forties, but apparently his arteries were really blocked. He just fell down in the middle of a game and died right there on the court."

I shuddered. "How old was Jo's husband?"

"Only thirty-seven," Aunt Evie said, shaking her head sadly. "He was a lovely man, too. Such a tragedy."

CHAPTER 23

ON FRIDAY MORNING, I WOKE WITH A SENSE OF ANTICIPATION. Today I would pick up my new car. Of course that was what was causing the excitement bubbling behind my rib cage. Not the prospect of spending an hour in a car with the delectable Curtis Kane and his sweet daughter.

My good mood was soured only slightly by the ring of the doorbell. Right on time. Steve was so reliable. With a sigh, I relieved him of Will's latest floral offering and resolved to walk them straight over to Sunrise Lodge. Maybe if Aunt Evie didn't want any more flowers, I could give them to Neville instead.

If only Will would give up this ridiculous idea of romancing me into changing my mind. Couldn't he see that every unwanted bouquet only hardened my resolve? Curtis was right—this was bordering on harassment now. I whiled away the walk with a pleasant daydream of Curtis slapping Will in handcuffs and taking him away in the back of a patrol car.

On the way, I stopped at the bakery and grabbed a bag of doughnuts. The pink icing reminded me of Maisie and I smiled. Hopefully, Aunt Evie would like them as much as that young lady did. I wasn't above offering bribes to get her to take the flowers off my hands.

As I strolled up the driveway at Sunrise Lodge, a ute roared past me, doing far more than the posted speed limit of ten kilometres an hour. The driver parked—badly —outside the Harrington apartment block, taking up two parking spots instead of one. A familiar bulky figure got out and slammed the door.

Larry didn't see me, but I watched as he took a toolbox out of the tray of the ute and strode toward the Harrington. My heart began to pound uncomfortably in my chest. Clearly he was going to visit his father-in-law—but was he playing the dutiful son-in-law and doing some sort of odd job for him, or was there a more sinister reason for that box of tools? Visions of Neville lying on the floor, his snowy white hair caked with blood and a wrench abandoned on the floor beside him, rose in my mind.

I stopped. My feet just wouldn't take me any further. My whole mind filled with visions of violence. *This is crazy, Charlie. Can't a man visit his own father-in-law without bystanders assuming he's there to commit murder?* But I'd got such a bad vibe from Larry. I could see those meaty hands clenched around a hammer or a wrench perfectly well. What should I do?

I dropped the flowers on the pavement at my feet and pulled out my phone. Aunt Evie answered on the third ring.

"Are you busy right now?" I asked, not bothering with the niceties.

She picked up immediately on the tension in my voice. "No, not at all. What's wrong?"

"Uh ... Probably nothing, but can you meet me at the Harrington right now?"

"Of course. I'll be there in a jiffy." No questions asked, just instant readiness to drop everything. I loved her for always being there for me.

She hung up. I put away my phone and picked up the flowers again. I should have just gone in there without her. What if my delay cost Neville his life? Surely no one in their right mind would carry out a murder with a witness knocking on the front door?

No one in their right mind goes around murdering people.

That was true. And I wouldn't put anything past the sour-faced Larry. Maybe I was a coward, but I was too afraid to confront him without backup. Aunt Evie wasn't much physically, but she was a warrior at heart and not even Larry could do us both in at the same time.

She appeared a moment later, walking briskly toward me. I'd never been so glad to see her. I started moving toward the courtyard of the Harrington block straight away.

"What's wrong?" she asked as she joined me. "You look so pale. Are you sick?"

"I'm fine. Here, hold these." I thrust the flower arrangement at her. Better to have my hands free. "I just saw Larry Brandt heading towards Neville's apartment with a box of tools."

She gave me a blank look. "So?"

"So, what if he's the murderer? He could be heading there right now to finish off what he started at the wedding."

"Goodness! So you think he's the killer?"

We passed into the shaded interior of the Harrington's courtyard. "I can't think of anyone else with a better motive. Maybe I'm imagining things, but I'm scared for Neville."

Aunt Evie actually grinned. "I'm so glad you moved to Sunrise Bay, darling. Things were never this exciting before you arrived."

I rolled my eyes. *Exciting* wasn't the word I would have picked. Aunt Evie actually seemed to be enjoying herself as she marched along beside me, brandishing her pink roses. Now that she was here, I felt a little calmer. Surely this was all in my head? People didn't really go around hitting sweet old men in the head with hammers in broad daylight, did they?

"Go on, then, darling," Aunt Evie said, as I stopped outside Neville's door. "What are you waiting for?"

I listened, but I couldn't hear any sounds of violence and mayhem. All my fears surged up again, convinced that was an eerie silence.

"What if he's already dead?" I whispered.

"Oxford's Law says he's not," Aunt Evie said bracingly.

I sighed. "It's Occam's Razor."

She smirked, and I realised she'd said it wrong on purpose to tease me. "If they wanted people to remember it, they shouldn't have given it such a stupid name."

"It's named after the guy who proposed it! He was a monk."

"Well, he should have taken a sensible monk name like Francis or Benedict. Or Peter. Peter's a nice name."

I shook my head in disbelief. There was absolutely no point telling her his name was William of Occam in her present mood. I raised my hand to knock.

"It's perfectly safe, darling. I'm sure Larry's not going to murder all three of us. Just get it over with quick, like ripping off a Band-Aid."

I rapped on the screen door. "Neville?" I called. "Are you there?" The door bounced as I knocked. It wasn't even latched, so I opened it and pushed on the main front door. That gave, too. "Hello? Is anyone there?"

"Hello," a voice called, and I heaved a huge sigh of relief. It was Neville. I pushed the door open a little further and saw him making his careful way across the carpet towards us, leaning on his walking stick. A bright smile of greeting spread across his wizened face.

"This is a lovely surprise. Look, Larry. We have two beautiful ladies visiting us."

I became aware of the sound of an electric drill in the kitchen just as it cut off. Larry poked his big head around the corner and scowled when he saw us.

Aunt Evie breezed past him and flicked the switch on the kettle. Good thinking. We should hang around until Larry finished whatever job he was doing. Just in case. I was reassured to see Neville so hale and hearty, but I wouldn't take any chances.

I swung the backpack off my shoulder and dug out the

bag of doughnuts, now slightly squished. "I brought some morning tea."

"And flowers!" Aunt Evie called from the kitchen, clearly enjoying herself hugely.

"I hope you like doughnuts."

"I like anything I don't have to cook myself," Neville said. "Are they from Jenny's Bakery?"

His eyes lit up when I said they were.

By now the kettle was bubbling merrily and Aunt Evie was rattling around the kitchen, getting out cups and plates, by the sounds of it. "Would you like some tea, too, dear?" she asked Larry.

"I don't drink tea," he replied, with all his usual grace.

Meanwhile, Neville was tottering toward the dining table where Aunt Evie had left the flowers, fussing about the mess on it. His idea of mess was totally different to his daughter's. Apart from the flowers, the only things on it were a couple of pens, what looked like a shopping list, and a birthday card that he must have been writing in when we arrived.

"Don't worry about that," I begged him as he swept it out of the way with shaking hands. "We didn't mean to inconvenience you. I was coming to visit Aunt Evie and then I just ..."

Just what, Charlie? Just saw your grumpy son-in-law popping in for a visit and decided to check he wasn't hurrying up his wife's inheritance? "I just thought you might enjoy doughnuts, too."

It sounded lame to my ears, but Neville looked

delighted. "I like the jam-filled ones best," he confided. "I don't suppose you have any of those?"

I moved into the kitchen, which was getting rather crowded now with three of us in it, looking for a plate to put the doughnuts on. Larry was fiddling with the hinges on one of the cupboard doors. Perhaps the door had been sagging. He gave me a sour look as I squeezed past his bulk.

"No jam ones, I'm afraid," I called back to Neville. "I have a couple of cinnamon and some pink iced and choco-late iced ones."

"Never mind. A man would have to be mad to say no to a chocolate iced doughnut," Neville said.

The kettle boiled and cut off. Larry's drill whirred again and the smell of sawdust floated on the air. Aunt Evie bustled around the tiny kitchen, digging tea and sugar out of cupboards. She already had three cups lined up on the bench.

"How do you take your tea?" she asked Neville.

"Snow white and two dwarves, please."

She added two generous spoons of sugar to his cup while Larry packed his drill back into his toolbox. He swung the cupboard door a couple of times to test it, then slammed it shut. "All good now, Neville."

"Thank you," Neville said. "That's been driving me crazy. Are you sure you wouldn't like to stay for a cuppa?"

"Some of us have to work," Larry grouched, before stomping his way to the front door. My nerves finally calmed when he banged it shut behind him.

"Well, this is lovely," Neville said as Aunt Evie and I

brought the tea and doughnuts to the table. "It's a regular little tea party. And all the better for being so unexpected."

"Surprises are fun," Aunt Evie agreed as she took her seat. Then she glanced at me. "Good ones, at least."

Oh, no. I knew what the next thing out of her mouth was going to be.

"Poor Charlie has been getting a lot of unwelcome ones lately." She indicated the enormous arrangement of roses on the table. And then she proceeded to fill Neville in on Will's attempts to win me back, including a recitation of his singing at the café which had grown rather large in the telling.

I focused on a chocolate doughnut and left her to it. Chocolate doughnuts were one of life's good surprises. As Neville said, a person would be mad to turn one down.

CHAPTER 24

Curtis knocked on the door promptly at ten past three on Friday afternoon. He'd had to wait until Maisie finished school, but he'd had the car all packed and ready to go with her things, so all they had to do once he'd picked her up was drive over to collect me.

I snatched the door open while his hand was still raised from knocking. "I'm ready," I said, a little breathlessly.

He grinned. "There's no hurry. I know Newcastle's an hour away, but we have plenty of time to get you to the dealership before they shut."

"I know, I know." The dealership was open until six o'clock, as I'd told him when we were making our arrangements. "I'm just excited to see my new car."

And I *was* a little excited about getting a car back. These weeks of walking around or relying on other people's kindness had shown me the independence your own set of wheels gave you. But maybe that wasn't the entire reason for my excitement. No need for Curtis to know that, of course.

Maisie waved vigorously from her booster seat as we walked down the drive toward Curtis's car. When he wasn't in a patrol car, Curtis drove a small white four-wheel-drive with roof racks. Living around here, that probably meant he was a surfer or a fisherman. He opened the passenger door for me and I slid in, a little bemused at the star treatment. Will had never opened a door for me in his life.

"Hi, Charlie," Maisie squeaked. "We've got snakes!"

She held up a bag of snake lollies which was already open. A bright green jelly snake lolled precariously out the side of the packet.

"Did you start eating them without us?" Curtis asked as he started the engine. "They were meant to be for the trip."

"*My* trip started when we left school, Daddy."

He rolled his eyes at her in the mirror. "I swear this kid is going to be a lawyer one day, Charlie."

"Then I could put the bad guys in jail after you catch them," she said.

I smiled, relaxing into my seat. "Sounds like a perfect plan."

Curtis grinned at me as he turned onto the road that led out of Sunrise Bay. "There's nothing like teamwork, is there?"

I agreed. Team Curtis and Maisie sounded like a great team to be on.

Curtis was easy to talk to, and Maisie was a lot of fun.

We played a game of I Spy for part of the trip that was only slightly hampered by the fact that Maisie's grasp on the alphabet wasn't entirely sure. It took Curtis a good five minutes to convince her that "cinema" didn't start with an "s".

"How about a new game?" I asked once the argument had subsided. "It's like I Spy, but the answer is always *a tree*." And there were plenty of trees along the side of the highway.

"That doesn't sound very fun," Maisie said doubtfully.

"The fun part is that you have to think up a new way to describe a tree every time. I'll go first. I spy with my little eye something brown and green."

"A tree," Curtis said.

"Okay, your turn."

"I spy with my little eye something that has leaves and branches."

"A tree!" Maisie shouted, getting into the spirit of the game.

After a while it got harder to think of ways to describe a tree, but we all enjoyed shouting "a tree!" every time. We played for about fifteen minutes, then we declared Maisie the winner for, "I spy with my little eye something that dogs like to wee on".

But about halfway through the trip, the steady hum of the engine and the long straight freeway with nothing to look at but trees lulled the little girl into slumber.

"Maisie's asleep," I said, checking her over my shoulder. "She looks so uncomfortable."

Her head was tipped right back against the side of her

booster seat, her mouth open. If I slept like that I'd have a crick in my neck for a week afterwards.

Curtis checked in the rear vision mirror and grinned. "She'll be all right. She's got my talent for falling asleep anywhere."

"She's a lovely kid," I said. "You should be very proud of her."

"I am." A shadow crossed his face. "She handled the divorce like a trooper. But I miss coming home to her every night."

"How often do you see her?"

"It started out as every second weekend, plus Tuesday nights, but it's kind of a movable feast these days between my shift work and Kelly's modelling jobs. We work it out as we go along."

"Does Kelly travel a lot for her modelling?"

"She's often away for four or five days at a time for a shoot. Or a shoot and a bit of a holiday. She spends a lot of time with this new guy she's hooked up with. Sometimes she seems to forget she has a reason to come home. Kelly likes the party life."

There was a definite sour note in his voice.

"But that means more time for you with Maisie, doesn't it? Isn't that a good thing?"

"Well, you'd think so, but she's also spiteful. She knows how much I miss Maisie, so rather than just let me have her when she's busy, she often leaves her with her grandma. So the poor kid's getting dragged around between three houses instead of two." He glanced across at me with a rueful smile. "Still, you don't want to hear about my custody squabbles. Let's talk about something else."

I was actually quite interested in his custody squabbles. I hadn't met the mysterious Kelly, though I'd heard about her from one or two people. But clearly it was a sore topic for him, so we started talking about movies we'd seen instead. The miles flew by in conversation, and before I knew it we were entering the outskirts of Newcastle.

"I never asked you what kind of car you're getting," Curtis said.

"Same as before, a Mazda 3. I had a new for old replacement insurance policy, so I'm just getting the same thing again. Though this time I've ordered a red one."

He grinned across at me. "I hear those red ones go faster. I hope I won't end up catching you speeding one day."

I laughed. "I think I'll be pretty safe. I'll probably be driving like a granny for a few weeks at least, until I get my confidence back."

We stopped at a set of lights, the first one since we'd left Sunrise Bay, and he eyed me thoughtfully. "Are you worried about driving again? Lots of people do find it tough to get back behind the wheel after an accident."

"I'm sure I'll be fine. My aunt bullied me into driving her car the other day, so it's not as though this will be my first time."

His eyes still rested on me, showing a warm concern. The car behind us tooted and he jerked his gaze back to the lights, which had changed to green. "How are you, after your accident, anyway?"

"I'm fine. All healed up."

"I don't mean just the whiplash, I mean in general. Mentally, emotionally. That was a pretty scary experience for you."

I was touched by his thoughtfulness. "Honestly, I try not to think about it." I couldn't quite repress a shudder, but his eyes were on the road again so he didn't notice. "It wasn't exactly a great welcome to Sunrise Bay, but I was lucky. It was only the car that got destroyed, and cars are replaceable."

"True. That's a good way of looking at it. I've seen some shocking car crashes in my time on the force. Some that people haven't walked away from. It's a devastating thing."

"It must be a tough job, being a first responder. Turning up to a crash and never knowing what you'll find."

"The craziest part is, you can never really predict it. There was one crash I attended where my heart sank into my boots when we pulled up. The car was wrapped around a telegraph pole and I'm just looking at it and thinking, there is no *way* anybody is still alive in there. And then we get out of the car and this bloke walks over to us. He's just been sitting on the side of the road waiting for us to turn up. Not a scratch on him."

"And he was in the car?"

"He was the driver. The airbag saved him. He said the

hardest part was forcing the door open." He shook his head in wonder at the memory.

"I'm a big fan of airbags myself, these days."

We stopped at another set of lights, and up ahead on the left I saw the Mazda dealership.

"And yet, other times, people seem fine at first and then everything goes pear-shaped. I got called to a two-car accident last year. An old guy T-bones another car. He was a little shaken up but otherwise fine. The other driver had a broken arm. It didn't seem anything major. Didn't even need an ambo—just got his wife to drive him to hospital. Reasonably young guy, too. I heard later that he died on the operating table."

I stared at him, hardly noticing as he slowed for the turn into the Mazda dealership. My mind was busy assembling a worrying jigsaw out of some very strange pieces.

Maisie woke up when the car stopped and looked around blearily. "Are we here already?" She pouted a little as she met my eyes. "I wanted to play another game of I Spy a Tree with Charlie."

My mind was still whirring as I opened the door. Could it be? I didn't want to believe it, but stranger things had happened.

"Charlie has to go now," Curtis said. "She's got to pick up her new car and get home again. And we have to get *you* to Mum's hotel in time for dinner."

"Thanks so much for the ride," I said.

"You're welcome." He smiled that warm smile of his, but I hardly even noticed the dimple, which proved how distracted I was. "Drive carefully."

"Always do," I said automatically. "Bye, Maisie!"

"Bye, Charlie, I love you!" she shouted as I closed the door.

Curtis waved, then drove off. I stared after the car, a terrible weight lodged in my stomach that had nothing to do with the prospect of driving my new car home.

CHAPTER 25

I TOSSED AND TURNED HALF THE NIGHT, HORRIFIED BY THE connections my brain was making. Surely I was wrong. I couldn't bear to think I was right. I stared at the card Curtis had given me a few weeks ago, with his phone number on it. I even entered it into my contacts and then stared at the screen instead, my finger hovering, ready to make that call. Would he think I was crazy, or would he leap into action? I so wanted to be wrong but I was very afraid that I wasn't.

About three o'clock in the morning I decided I needed more information before I went to the police with this. Eventually I fell into a weary slumber and woke just after eight with a thundering headache.

I dragged myself into the shower, then liberally applied coffee. The headache eased back from thundering to merely annoying and I got behind the wheel of my shiny new red car. By nine-thirty I was outside the doors of Randall Clifford's shop.

The bell chimed its discreet melodious note as I opened the door but no one greeted me. The shop was empty. I stopped in the middle of the floor, bemused.

The workshop door opened abruptly and Randall Clifford himself appeared. His welcoming expression cooled somewhat when he saw it was me. "Good morning. I didn't expect to see you back here so soon."

"I have a couple more questions for you."

His expression was rapidly approaching Arctic. "Not about the cyanide, surely? The police were fully satisfied with my explanations and I don't really see what business it is of yours."

"It's not, exactly," I admitted, "but I'm concerned that it really *is* business of yours. Tell me, does anyone else have access to that key you were telling me about the other day? The one for locking up your cyanide?"

He drew himself up straighter. "As I told you before, I keep the keys on my person."

"At all times? Are you sure? There's never a time, say, when you leave them on the workbench in your studio and just duck out for a coffee or to go to the bathroom? Isn't it possible that one of the staff might have had access? Someone could have made a copy of the key if they found it unattended for a few minutes. And what about break-ins?" *Please, let there have been a break-in.* "Have you ever been broken into here? Could someone have stolen cyanide as well as jewels?"

He huffed out an exaggerated sigh of annoyance. "I can see I'm not going to get any peace from you until I convince you that you are barking up the wrong tree. We have never had a break-in here in the whole twelve years we've been in these premises. And my staff are all hand-picked, honest and trustworthy. Even if I did occasionally leave the keys in the workshop for a moment, I can assure you that none of them would be sneaking around making copies. Now, does that satisfy your infernal curiosity?"

"Just one more question. Where's Jo today? I thought she worked here full-time."

His tight expression eased now that the topic of cyanide seemed to be closed. "Oh, she's working. She's just ducked out to make a delivery. I had a commission for a special birthday and the customer needs it today. But he can't drive and his lift fell through, so I said it was no trouble, we would deliver. We pride ourselves on our exceptional service."

An uneasy sensation tightened my belly. "The customer isn't Neville Botham, is it?"

"I'm afraid that's private information," he said primly, but it was too late. The flicker of surprise on his face had answered the question for him.

The uneasiness in my gut spiked into full-blown panic. "How long ago did she leave?"

"You just missed her. No more than five minutes or so."

I spun on my heel and wrenched open the door. "Thanks," I called back into his surprised face and literally ran down the street to where I'd left the car.

I leapt in and started the engine, and had a moment's sheer panic when I couldn't find the handbrake, before remembering that this model had a tiny little finger-sized lever instead. I took off down the street and headed for Sunrise Lodge, doing way more than the fifty-kilometres-an-hour speed limit. Curtis would get a real shock if he caught me speeding already on only my second day with the car.

Curtis! I should ring him. My heart pounded and I took a couple of deep breaths, trying to force the panic down. I was no use to Neville if I ended up wrapped around a tree.

I'd thrown my bag on the floor on the passenger side and now I couldn't reach my phone. And I hadn't taken the time yet to read the manual to figure out how to connect the phone to the car Bluetooth. For the first time in my life, I was praying for the police to catch me speeding. At least then I could get some help for Neville.

What if he was already dead? She had a five-minute start on me and five minutes was a long time to a determined killer. Neville was a pretty soft target—I could probably kill him myself in a couple of minutes, if I were the kind of person who went around murdering people.

I shuddered at the visions that arose in my mind of Neville, opening the door with that sweet, sunny smile. He'd be so thrilled to receive the jewellery he'd commissioned for Kim's fiftieth birthday, he wouldn't suspect a thing. And then he'd turn his back on her and bam! He'd be helpless. How would she do it? A knife? A blunt instrument? There was blood all over his walls in my mind, and my new steering wheel was slippery with the sweat of my fear.

I leapt out of the car outside the Harrington building, pausing only to grab my handbag and snatch the phone out of it as I rushed through the green, shaded garden.

Please answer please answer please answer.

"Curtis here." His deep voice was calm, friendly.

"It's me, Charlie," I gasped.

"You sound like you've been running." I could hear the smile in his voice. "Don't tell me that new car of yours has broken down already?"

"I need your help." Neville's front door was in sight. It was closed.

"What's wrong?"

"I'm at the Harrington apartments at Sunrise Lodge. Please, can you come? I'm afraid the killer is about to strike again. It's Neville." This was coming out so disjointed, my tongue tripping over itself in my rush. "Neville Botham. He lives at number ninety-eight. Please hurry."

"Neville Botham is the killer?"

"No, no! She's after him. Jo. Jo London. It was him she meant to kill at the wedding, but they swapped meals and she got Ben Cassar instead. Oh, please hurry. She's going to kill him, I know it. She thinks it's all his fault that her husband died."

"I'll be two minutes." He was all brisk competence now. "Don't do anything until I get there."

CHAPTER 26

There was no sign of Jo, or Neville either. My heart pounded in my throat as I reached for the handle of the screen door. If she was five minutes ahead of me … But Neville was always slow to answer the door. Maybe I was still in time. My hand closed around the handle and turned. Not locked. Neither was the main door. I threw it open, not bothering to knock. If they were sitting there drinking tea together and discussing Neville's purchase I would look like a fool, but at this point I didn't care.

They weren't drinking tea.

"Stop it!" I screamed.

Neville was flat on his back on the lounge room floor, his skinny arms and legs splayed wide. Jo crouched over him, leaning all her body weight into the cushion she had over his face. Her tear-streaked face was a snarl of rage as she looked at me over her shoulder.

"Get off him!" I hurled my bag aside and grabbed her by the arm, trying to drag her away. She fought back, desperate to complete the job. Had she killed him already? He lay so horribly still. She was strong for a small woman and slapped me so hard across the cheek that my ears rang.

But I managed to kick the cushion away from Neville's face as she lunged at me, hands crooked into claws, fury in her face. "Why do you keep sticking your nose in? You're ruining everything!"

I sidestepped neatly and circled to keep myself between her and Neville. She grabbed a photo frame from the top of a display cabinet and hurled it at me. I didn't quite manage to duck it. That would be another bruise. She looked around for something else to throw but Neville's house was neat and the coasters on his dining table didn't seem to do anything for her.

"Stop and think, Jo," I said, trying to keep my voice calm and steady, though inside I was quaking. "It's too late. You can't get away with this. You're only making it worse."

She cast around desperately and her eyes lit on the knife block on the kitchen bench. Oh, no. I was in trouble now.

She grabbed the biggest one and came at me with the determination of madness in her eyes. I snatched up the cushion from the floor by Neville's head, wishing I had a better shield. I would have run, but then Neville would be here defenceless and I couldn't abandon him.

"You've already killed one person, Jo. This is madness. Xavier wouldn't have wanted you to do this. Put the knife down."

Where was Curtis? His two minutes were well and truly up. Nothing would sound more like music to my ears right now than the wail of a police siren.

"How do you know what Xavier would have wanted? You never met him." She still brandished the knife but at least she wasn't getting any closer. Maybe if I kept her talking I would be all right. "He died before his thirty-eighth birthday—and this useless waste of space is still hanging around taking up oxygen at *eighty*-eight." She gestured wildly at Neville's prone body with the knife, its sharp tip catching the light from the open door. "How is that fair? He was my everything. We had our whole lives planned. We were going to move to England and start a family. And now he's gone."

"I'm so sorry for your loss. I can't even imagine how hard that must have been. But killing Neville won't bring him back. It won't fix anything."

Clearly, that was the wrong thing to say. "Yes, it will," she snarled. "It's the injustice of it all. It's killing me. It's all I ever think about. Xavier comes to me in my dreams. He can't understand why I haven't made it right. I'll have no peace until I do."

She took another step toward me and I backed up. I couldn't go any further without stepping over Neville and I had to stay between them. She thought her dead husband was telling her to kill poor Neville. The woman needed mental help, but first I had to stop her. "Put the knife down," I said again. "Let's talk about this like reasonable people."

"No. Enough talking. It's time for action now. I

219

shouldn't have waited so long, but I was scared. Did you know they didn't even charge him? He killed my Xavier, and all they did was take away his stupid licence. How does that help Xavier find peace? I'm the only one that can help him now."

She lunged at me, the knife upraised. I squealed and tried to deflect it with the cushion. This was not how I had imagined my new life in peaceful Sunrise Bay. But somehow I got lucky and the knife caught in the stuffing. I hurled the cushion away with the knife still stuck in it, and then it was just me and her.

"Get out of my way!" she screamed in frustration.

Pounding footsteps in the courtyard outside heralded a new arrival. "Charlie, get behind me."

Thank God, it was Curtis.

"You called the police?" Jo whirled away and plucked another knife from the knife block. "I hate you. Why can't you keep out of other people's business? I thought I had plenty of time to plan another attempt, then you came snooping around asking about cyanide."

Curtis strode farther into the room, his hands empty and held wide in a placating gesture. He was in plain clothes, barefoot. He must have been off duty and leapt into his car at my call. "Jo, how about you come outside with me and we talk about this?"

He gave my shoulder a reassuring squeeze as he reached my side and I stepped back gratefully, letting him take over. Just having his presence in the room made me feel calmer. He hadn't stopped for shoes, but he'd taken long enough to buckle on his gun belt. The gun was still holstered but I felt better knowing he could defend himself if necessary. I trusted him not to use it unless he had to.

"Go outside and wait for the ambulance," he said in a low tone. "I called it in. Back-up will be here any minute."

I retreated to give him more room but I wasn't going anywhere, not with Neville still stretched out on the carpet like that. I crouched down and felt for a pulse in his wrinkled neck. It was weak, but mercifully still there. I stroked his snowy hair, heart still full of fear for him.

"Give me the knife, Jo. You don't want to do this."

"Yes, I do." Her voice was raw with angry tears. "I should have done it months ago, but I was too weak. Too scared."

"No, you weren't. You were grieving, and that's perfectly natural. But violence doesn't solve anything. You'll feel better if we talk about it." He looked so solid and dependable, and there was nothing but gentle concern in his face. I didn't know how he could stay so calm.

"There's nothing to talk about." The tip of the knife wavered and then turned until it was resting against her own chest, roughly above her heart.

My pulse skyrocketed, but Curtis didn't seem ruffled. "Your husband wouldn't want you to hurt yourself, Jo."

"Don't come any closer or I'll kill myself," she warned. Curtis took no notice, continuing to move slowly forward until he was almost within arm's reach. "I mean it," she said. Her hands were steady on the knife hilt, though mine were shaking as I clutched Neville's hand between them.

In a blur of movement, Curtis leapt forward and grabbed her arms. In a moment, he had wrestled the knife out of her hand and hurled it across the room. Jo struggled violently against his grip then burst out in furious weeping and collapsed against his chest. His arms came around her, big hands stroking her back as he murmured soothingly to her. He caught my eye over her head and nodded, and I rose and went outside to direct the paramedics. Coming closer, I heard, at last, the wail of a police siren.

A package lay on the floor by the door, a black bag with the name of Randall's shop inscribed in elegant silver cursive on the side. Half spilled out of it was a red velvet jewellery box, which must have been the gift for Kim.

It didn't matter what was in that box or how much it had cost her doting father. I was sure the best gift she could possibly receive for her fiftieth birthday would be knowing that her father had survived.

CHAPTER 27

I<small>T WAS ALMOST DARK BY THE TIME</small> I <small>GOT HOME</small>. I'<small>D SPENT A</small>
couple of hours at the police station making a statement
to a very disgruntled Detective McGovern, who didn't
seem at all grateful that I had solved his case for him. And
I didn't even say *I told you so* once, which I felt showed
remarkable restraint on my part.

After Curtis had driven me back to Sunrise Lodge to
get my car, Aunt Evie and I had had lunch together. A nice
pot of Earl Grey tea had finally calmed my jittery nerves.
Talking it all over with Aunt Evie helped, too. In the afternoon we dropped in at the hospital to see Neville, who
was being kept overnight for observation. Nothing was
broken, thankfully, but his old bones had not enjoyed the
tumble to the floor when Jo attacked him, and he was a
mass of aches and pains.

"But I'm lucky to be alive at all," he'd said. The dramas
of the morning hadn't dimmed the wattage of his

beaming smile. "It was a lucky day for me that I met you, young lady. I can't thank you enough."

When I pulled into my driveway at dusk, Rufus ambled over to greet me with a lazy wag of his feathery tail.

"Hello, beautiful." I bent down to stroke his silky head and rubbed vigorously behind his ears. "Who's a gorgeous boy? That's right! You are! *You're* a gorgeous boy." I unlocked my front door, still babbling nonsense to him. I didn't know what it was about dogs that always made people want to baby-talk to them, but I had a bad case of it. "Are you hungry? Want some yummy kibble?"

As well as the chew toys, the flea treatment, and the new lead—oh, and the special grooming brush—I'd also invested in a giant bag of kibble, since Rufus seemed to spend more time in my house than Mrs Johnson's lately. It seemed rude not to feed him.

I flicked on the light and stopped. Red rose petals were scattered all over the floor in the foyer. Rufus sniffed dubiously at them, then sneezed. What on earth?

I closed the door behind me, uncertain. The petals formed a trail up the stairs as far as I could see. My heart began to beat a little faster. Someone had been in my house while I was out.

Moving very quietly I placed my handbag on the hall table and withdrew my phone. With Rufus's collar in one hand and my phone in the other, I made a quick tour of the downstairs rooms. No one was there. There was no suspicious rose petal activity, either. It was all centred on the stairs.

I stood at the bottom of them, tapping my phone thoughtfully against one cheek. I didn't like this one bit. The idea that someone else had been in my house was unnerving, even though I doubted someone with bad intentions would be strewing rose petals everywhere. For a moment I wished it was Curtis, but it wasn't Curtis's style at all. He would never break in to someone's house. He was a straight arrow, as Priya had once said.

I knew exactly whose style this was.

"Come on, boy." I started up the stairs, patting my leg to encourage Rufus to come up with me. I wasn't sure what I would find up there, but I felt the need for a little backup.

The red petals led me all the way up the stairs like giant bloodstains on the cream carpet. They smelled nice, but I was beyond appreciating their perfume. Now that I was over the shock of discovering someone had been in my house, anger was growing into a tight ball inside my chest. How *dared* he?

I followed the petal trail to my bedroom door and stopped there. My mouth fell open. I'd expected another flower display—probably something wildly extravagant, a veritable florist's shop heaped on my bed. Or perhaps a pile of chocolates and other gifts.

What I *hadn't* expected was to discover someone had remade my bed with pink satin sheets, and that that someone was now lying between them. Stark naked, if the number of garments abandoned on the floor were anything to go by.

"What the *flip* do you think you're doing?" The anger

had boiled up out of my chest and tightened my throat so that my voice came out hard and raspy. Rufus trotted over to the bed, sniffing at the rose petal trail.

"Welcome home, darling," Will said. He patted the pink satin beside him invitingly. "Why don't you take off those clothes and come and get comfortable with me?"

Rufus wasn't one to ignore an invitation like that. He launched himself onto the bed with a happy woof. Will recoiled but it was too late. Rufus's heavy paw landed right in Will's vulnerable lap.

"Aargh!" Will doubled over and clutched his delicate bits in pain.

Rufus barked again in reply, thinking it was a game. He bounced excitedly around the bed, ears flapping, his nails tearing at the smooth satin.

"For heaven's sake, Charlie, get this thing off me! You know I'm allergic to dogs." His eyes were watering, but I wasn't sure if that was from his allergies or from the pain of copping a paw to the unmentionables.

"Rufus, come here." I patted my leg. He took a flying leap from the bed and trotted over to me, his tail wagging proudly. My hero. "Good boy."

"Since when have you had a dog?" Will hunched defensively over himself, the satin sheet pulled up tight around his chest.

"Really? That's what you want to talk about?" I couldn't believe the gall of the man. He'd slept with my best friend. He'd lied to me and betrayed me. Now he was breaking into my house as if he had every right to be there but he wanted to complain about a pet? "The dog is not the problem here, Will. You are. Have you completely lost your mind?"

His eyes were still watering. "It's fine. If you must have a dog, I'm sure we can work something out."

"Work something out? Are you crazy? Will, get out of my bed. There is nothing to work out because there is no 'us' anymore. I can have fifty dogs plus a goose and a horse and a—and a *pelican* if I want." I threw my arms around, imagining up a whole menagerie. "It has nothing to do with you. My *life* is nothing to do with you."

He threw back the sheet and got out of bed, still wincing as he started to pull on his pants. Of course, they were balled up in the corner of the room, just the way he used to do when we lived together. It had driven me mad. Why had I put up with it for so long?

I folded my arms and watched him dancing around on one foot trying to get his pants on, and felt absolutely liberated that his discarded clothes were no longer my problem. Until that moment, I hadn't realised how much I'd been enjoying having a neat bedroom.

"Your life has everything to do with me. We're engaged."

Was I hearing right? Will had always had an amazing capacity to ignore inconvenient facts, but this was taking things to extremes. "No, we're not. I threw that engagement ring back at you the night I found you in bed with Amy. It's over, Will, and it's been over for weeks. You have to leave me alone now. This has gone too far—now you're breaking and entering."

"Nonsense." He zipped up his pants and bent for his T-shirt. "I didn't break anything. The old woman next door let me in."

My eyebrows rose. Mrs Johnson and I would have to have a chat. "What on earth for?"

We had swapped front door keys not long after I'd arrived. She had seemed so concerned that she might one day lock herself out and need a spare key somewhere handy. I'd thought it was a good idea and had given her a copy of mine, too, but I hadn't expected her to use it to let undesirables into my house.

"I told her I was your boyfriend, come up from Sydney to surprise you."

I sighed. Mrs Johnson had heard me complain enough times about Will's flowers to realise he was not my boyfriend. Perhaps she had a secret romantic streak and thought she was helping the course of true love run smooth. If so, she was rooting for the wrong team.

"I didn't mean to upset you," Will said as his head emerged from his T-shirt. "I thought this would be romantic."

"Romantic! Absolutely not. It's *creepy*. You can't just go around breaking into"—he opened his mouth to protest and I amended it—"all right, conning innocent neighbours into *letting* you into people's houses. Can't you see this is wrong?"

He threw his arms in the air in frustration. "The only thing I see here that's wrong is that you aren't with me anymore. Babe, you've got no idea how much I miss you. Look, I'm sorry I've messed this all up. I've never been very good at romance, but for you I'm willing to try."

My heart was almost touched at the pathetic expression in his eyes, and then I found my backbone and hardened up again. I had faced down a knife-wielding killer. I refused to yield to Will's feeble attempts to manipulate me anymore. "You're willing to try to romance me,"—I made imaginary quote marks in the air around the words *romance me*—"with stupid gestures, but you're not willing to be faithful to me if a better opportunity presents itself? That's not love, Will, and that's not what I want. This is over and if you can't see that, I suggest you need professional help."

He crossed the floor in two quick strides and grabbed my arms. "But don't you miss it? Don't you miss what we had? I made a mistake, I realise that now, and I'm sorry, but you can't hold it against me forever."

"Oh, yes, I can. There are some mistakes there's no coming back from and I'd say sleeping with your fiancée's best friend is one of them. Now let *go*."

I tried to pull away, but he wouldn't release me. In typical Will style, he tried to draw me into a hug instead. Well, I wasn't having that.

"Will, enough!" I shouted, my temper finally boiling over. Rufus barked and rushed to my side as I wrenched myself out of Will's grasp. "Get out of my house. If you come near me again I'm calling the police and getting a restraining order."

He opened his mouth to argue again, and Rufus growled. Surprised, I looked down at him. I'd never heard him growl before. He was usually such a happy, friendly animal. But clearly he'd decided that Will was not a person he wished to be friends with, and he placed himself in front of me, ready to guard me from the threat.

Not that Will presented any great threat. As soon as Rufus growled, he stepped back hurriedly.

"Fine, fine. I'll go." He snatched up his shoes and socks from the floor and backed carefully out of the room. Rufus barked again, obviously pleased with his sudden power over the enemy, and Will lost his nerve entirely. He turned at the top of the stairs and almost flew down the steps, the sound of Rufus's triumphant barking chasing him out of the house.

The front door slammed, and I sat down on the bed. "Good boy, Rufus. Good boy." I stroked his soft head and he sat down, his tail thumping lazily against the carpet and his eyes slowly closing in delight at the attention. "You deserve an extra treat tonight."

Chocolate brown eyes popped open again. "Oh, you know that word, do you? Treat? Would you like a treat *now*?"

He leapt up and ran to the door where he stood wagging, looking back at me expectantly. I laughed. "Okay, I can take a hint."

I followed him down the stairs, pausing only to make sure the front door was locked. I didn't need any more surprises today. Then I went into the kitchen and dug out some of the liver treats that Rufus liked so much.

"Would you like to stay here tonight, boy? You can sleep on my bed."

Just as soon as I stripped those stupid satin sheets off it.

CHAPTER 28

NEXT MORNING, I WAS SITTING IN MY SUNNY COURTYARD EATING breakfast when there was a knock at the front door. Rufus lifted his head and looked vaguely in that direction, then dropped it back down onto the warm pavers, as if it was just too much effort to hold it up.

"Some guard dog you are," I said as I went inside to see who was at the door. Maybe it was Curtis. He'd been around here on a Sunday before, and it would certainly be like him to come over to see how I was doing after the dramas of yesterday. A warmth filled me at the idea of finding that gorgeous policeman on my front doorstep.

But I was doomed to disappointment. It wasn't Curtis at all but Mrs Johnson, and she was holding two dog bowls and a half-empty bag of dog food in her arms.

"Hello," I said. "What's all this?" I opened the door wider and stepped back so she could come in. "Here, let me take that, it looks heavy." It was one of those giant bags of dog food, the budget kind. I dumped it on the kitchen bench and she put the two dog bowls next to it.

Rufus got up when he saw who it was and wandered in to say hello, his tail wagging lazily.

"I thought I'd find him here." She bent down and gave him a perfunctory pat. "It's perfectly clear he likes you more than me, dear. He spends more time at your place now than he does at mine."

A pang of guilt pierced me. I did so love Rufus's company, but maybe Mrs Johnson was lonely without him, even though she said she really wasn't a dog person. "I'm sorry. I know he's stayed here a couple of times overnight, but I didn't want to disturb you bringing him home. I know you like to go to bed early."

She patted my arm reassuringly. "Don't worry about it. It's perfectly fine by me. I just thought if he was going to stay with you, you might as well have all his bits and bobs. I have a bed for him, too, but it's a little heavy for me. You'll have to come and get that yourself."

I wasn't quite sure what she was offering. "But ... But he's your dog. I can't take him away from you. I only meant to borrow him a little, now and then. He's such a sweetheart." I glanced down at his big stupid face and couldn't help smiling at the happy, dopey look he was giving me. When his tongue lolled out like that he always looked like he was grinning. "I can't deprive you of your own dog."

She patted my arm again. "You're not depriving me of anything, dear. I'm giving him to you. Honestly, it would solve a big problem for me if you would take him off my hands. If I knew he had someone who really loved him to take care of him, I could move into Sunrise Lodge with a clear conscience. My sister Betty's in Ocean View there and she's been trying to get me to move in ever since Bert died."

"Really? You mean it?" Happiness blossomed in my heart. "I can have him?"

"You might as well. I'd say he's picked you already. He knows where he wants to be. This is just making it official." Her face softened as she smiled at me. "Bert would be so thrilled to know Rufus has found a new owner like you. He loved that dog."

"I don't know what to say. I'm so happy!" Impulsively, I threw my arms around her narrow shoulders and gave her a hug.

"Well, then," she said, "I'm glad that's settled. Did you sort things out with your young man last night?"

"Oh." I'd forgotten Mrs Johnson's part in last night's fiasco. "He's not my young man. I was a little surprised you let him in—I thought you knew that we'd broken up."

That was as close as I could go to reprimanding her for being so free with my key. Now that she'd given me Rufus, I could forgive her anything.

"His car was absolutely full of roses. I didn't have the heart to turn him away."

I hadn't seen his car when I came home—he must have parked it around the corner after he'd unloaded all the flowers. Very sneaky.

"He seems a very persistent young man," she added. "He wouldn't take no for an answer."

"Yes, that's been the problem. But I think I've finally gotten through to him now."

"That's good. Probably a good thing you had the chance to talk things over, then." She sounded as if she was congratulating herself on throwing us together—absolutely no contrition for having let a rose-destroying stalker into my house. My phone, which was on the table out in the courtyard, began to ring. "Well, I'll leave you to enjoy your Sunday morning. Just pop over later to pick up Rufus's bed."

She let herself out and I went to answer the phone. It was Curtis.

"Hi," I said, suddenly breathless at seeing his name on the screen.

"Hi. I was just checking how our crime-fighting superhero is this morning."

"I'm good." I could hear the smile in his voice, which brought an answering smile to my own face.

"Did you sleep all right? No nightmares?"

"Yes, I slept fine, thanks. I had Rufus snuggled up to me all night."

"Rufus?" He sounded surprised. Shocked, even.

A fiery blush roared up my cheeks and into my hairline as it occurred to me that he might think I meant a man.

"The dog," I gasped. "You remember him! I had him with me at the café the other day."

"Oh." Was that relief I heard? "You mean Mrs Johnson's dog?"

"Yes. No." I took a deep breath. *Pull yourself together, Charlie. You sound like a noodlehead.* Having a cute guy on the phone was no reason for all my brain cells to die simultaneously. "Actually, he's my dog, now. Mrs Johnson has just given him to me."

"Nice! Retrievers are such good dogs. I've been thinking about getting one for Maisie, maybe. She'd love a pet."

"They're great with kids."

"And speaking of Maisie ..." He paused. "We usually have breakfast together at the surf club café on the weekend, but since she's with her mum, I'll be eating on my own."

He paused again, and I looked at Rufus, my eyes wide. Was Curtis asking me out? Rufus sat down and scratched behind one ear, supremely indifferent to this major turning point in my love life.

"So, I was wondering," he went on when I said nothing, "whether you'd like to join me."

I jumped up and down on the spot, holding in a silent squeal of excitement. Rufus got up, tail wagging, ready to join in the celebration despite not understanding what was going on.

"I'd love to," I said, trying not to sound like a sixteen-year-old with stars in her eyes, but not doing a very good job. I'd already had breakfast, but that didn't matter. For Curtis, I'd eat breakfast twenty times over. "Do you mind if I bring my dog?"

"Of course not."

"Great! See you there in ten?"

"It's a date."

The word *date* had me flustered all over again, and I hardly knew what I said as I hung up the phone. But I managed to hold it together until he'd gone, and then I let out the squeal I'd been holding in. Rufus barked and jumped up, putting his front paws on my waist.

I grabbed hold of them and danced him around the courtyard, giddy with excitement. "I have a date with Curtis Kane," I sang, and he barked back at me. "Oh, it's all right, boy, you can come, too."

I rushed upstairs to put on something more respectable than the daggy old shorts and T-shirt I'd been wearing, humming to myself in happiness. All of a sudden, things were looking up. I had a new home, a successful business, new friends—and the world's cutest dog.

Plus, a date with Curtis Kane. Life didn't get much better than that.

THE END

Keep up to date with new releases, special deals and other book news by signing up for my newsletter at www. emeraldfinn.com.

Reviews and word of mouth are vital for any author's success. If you enjoyed *Veil, Vows and Vengeance*, please take a moment to leave a short review where you bought it. Just a few words sharing your thoughts on the book would be extremely helpful in spreading the word to other readers (and this author would be immensely grateful!).

Come and chat with me and other cozy mystery lovers in the friendly Facebook group A Pocketful of Cozies. We'd love to have you!

DON'T MISS BLONDES, BIKINIS AND BETRAYAL!

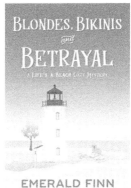

Turning thirty is murder

Everything's panning out for Charlie in picture-perfect Sunrise Bay. She has a new dog, a brand-new photography business, and maybe even a fresh romance with the hottest policeman in town. Plus, her latest photo shoot is double the fun. Identical twins Sam and Jess want photos to celebrate their thirtieth birthday.

But the party stops when Sam disappears. Rumours spread faster than you can say "cheese". Is her hot-tempered new boyfriend to blame? What did her neighbour really see?

When Sam's body is found in mysterious circumstances, Jess is distraught ... or is she? It's up to Charlie to sort fact from fiction in a puzzling case of double trouble.

Acknowledgements

Thanks, as always, to Jen Rasmussen for her brilliant editing and endless support. This woman is a legend and I'm so blessed to have her in my life.

Thanks also to my family for their love and support, especially my beautiful husband, who helped me in many practical ways, from plot discussions to beta reading to taking over the cooking so I could write. He is my biggest cheerleader and I love him to pieces, even if he thinks a balanced diet consists of steak, steak, and more steak.

About the Author

Emerald Finn loves books, tea, and chocolate, not necessarily in that order. Oh, and dogs. And solving mysteries with the aid of her trusty golden retriever. No, wait. That last bit might be made up.

In fact, Emerald herself is made up, though it's absolutely true that she loves books, tea, chocolate, and dogs. Emerald Finn is the pen name of Marina Finlayson, who writes books full of magic and adventure under her real name. She shares her Sydney home with three kids, a large collection of dragon statues, and the world's most understanding husband.

Made in United States
North Haven, CT
27 August 2022

23309376R00150